"So you did sleep with David Thorpe!"

Marc ignored Camira's outraged expression and continued insultingly, "But when you found out he wouldn't marry you, you dropped him flat! Is that why he looks at you like some thirst-crazed desert traveler?"

"I knew I shouldn't have told you anything!" Camira spat. "It's only set your fertile imagination going."

"Why not prove your innocence?" he drawled, eyes glinting.

"Do you really think I'd sleep with you to prove I hadn't slept with David— or anyone else?" she asked contemptuously.

Marc stood up. "I thought you might sleep with me because you wanted to," he said quietly. "Yes, wanted to." He grinned suddenly as she retreated a step. "Do you think I don't know that you want me, Camira?"

My Dear Innocent

by

LINDSAY ARMSTRONG

Harlequin Books

TORONTO • LONDON • LOS ANGELES • AMSTERDAM
SYDNEY • HAMBURG • PARIS • STOCKHOLM • ATHENS • TOKYO

Original hardcover edition published in 1981
by Mills & Boon Limited

ISBN 0-373-02497-5

Harlequin Romance first edition September 1982

CHAPTER ONE

CAMIRA JOHNSTON stared in disbelief across the paddock and then down at the tap in her hand. Not so much as a drop flowed from the tap, which was attached to a small tank. Also attached to the tank were two long rubber pipes which stretched in opposite directions, one towards her precious vegetable garden and the other towards the neighbouring property. This one was buried beneath the ground for most of its length and where it emerged on the other side of the dividing fence between the two properties, it was normally attached to a mechanical pump—a pump upon which Camira's whole fragile economy was dependent. For without the water it sent surging down the pipe she couldn't grow her vegetables. And without her vegetables her small rustic roadside stall might as well be shut down.

But she could see quite clearly in the still, early morning light that the pipe had been ripped up for part of its length and looped over the fence and the pump was sitting fairly and squarely in the middle of the paddock. Her paddock. And beyond the fence the sunlight danced and glittered playfully on the smooth surface of a well-filled dam. . . .

She gasped as a tremendous gust of anger shook her. For a long moment she battled with herself, her nails biting into the palms of her clenched fists, but the anger and the fear, although she did not admit this to herself, was too strong, and with a forceful gesture she crammed her battered, shabby straw hat on to her head and strode off across the paddock.

The dividing fence between the two properties proved no obstacle to her, clad as she was in jeans and with sturdy wellingtons on her feet—but, as she told herself grimly, in my present state of mind I'd have climbed it in an evening gown. Not that I ever wear evening gowns. . . . Oh! How could they?

She strode on, looking neither left nor right, unmoved by the smooth opulence that characterised this property and was in such contrast to her own. There were no sagging fences here, no ramshackle buildings. Everything was neat, well painted and well maintained. As if it had just been gone over with a new broom.

Which it has, of course, she muttered to herself grimly. It had always been the showplace of the district even before its new owners had taken residence, but now it was as if a glow had been added. The training track sported new fencing and the stables had been re-roofed. But it was the homestead that always took the eye, and now more so than ever. It was a gem of Queensland colonial architecture, a rambling wooden building with a steep roof and surrounded on all sides by a deep, cool verandah. The beautifully carved wooden 'lacework' that formed the verandah wall had been fully restored, and it was this that struck an even more bitter note in Camira's heart as she walked up the front steps.

She stopped on the top step and stared at the archway above her head with its intricately carved legend. The one word mocked her, or so it seemed to her overwrought nerves, and she clenched her fists once more and with gritted teeth advanced across the verandah and pounded on the heavy front door.

A dog barked from deep inside the house and she heard the sound of slow footsteps down the long central passageway. She raised her knuckles and rapped sharply on the door again.

'Coming!' The door swung open and a sleepy-eyed, tousled head appeared and regarded her blearily. 'Is there a fire? What's going on?'

Camira regarded the half-dressed figure frostily and realised it was a teenage boy with a freckled face and straight fair hair now dangling in his eyes. She assessed his age to be about fifteen and noted that he had his hand tucked into the collar of a large, ferocious-looking dog. But the dog wriggled out of his grasp and with a joyous bark flung himself at Camira.

The boy's blue eyes widened in disbelief as, at a sharp command from Camira, the dog sank down and wagged his tail vigorously.

She bent and patted his head. 'That's a good boy.' She lifted her head and said sternly, in no way mollified by the little incident, 'I want to speak to the owner of the place, the *new* owner, right this minute—and don't try and tell me he's not here, because I happen to know he arrived yesterday afternoon!' She folded her arms deliberately.

The boy blinked. 'That might not be such a good idea,' he said slowly and with a hint of amusement. 'Er . . . who are you anyway?'

'Don't worry about that,' Camira said fiercely. 'Will you get him or shall I? Does he use the main bedroom? Right!' And she marched down the passageway.

'Here!' the boy said indignantly. 'You can't just walk in!'

Camira turned back. 'Oh, can't I? Just watch me!'

A deep masculine voice intervened. 'What the hell's

going on? And who the devil are you?'

Camira swung round on her heel and took an unexpected breath.

The owner of the voice was standing in the middle of the passageway just in front of her. He was a tall man, clad only in a pair of blue denim jeans of which he was still buttoning the waistband. His bare feet had aided his soundless arrival on the scene.

But tousled as he was too and obviously just risen from bed, Camira knew instinctively that this was someone who would always make an impression. A fleeting upward glance showed her his thick dark hair and hazel eyes, a smooth tanned skin . . . for a second her eyes lingered on his wide shoulders and then dropped to his narrow hips, and for some reason she felt herself blush like a silly schoolgirl.

Oh, I know all about the likes of you, she told herself furiously. Smooth and sophisticated, an elegant image sweeping all before you, but underneath it, tough, strong and hard. . . . The thought brought her fresh anger.

'Are you Marcus Riley?' she demanded angrily.

He narrowed his eyes. 'Yes. Who are you?'

'I'm your next-door neighbour, mate,' she said grimly. 'And I've come to tell you just what I think of *you*. You pulled up my pipes and disconnected my pump like some . . . thief in the night. You didn't even have the common decency to come and tell me first! I. . . .'

'Just a minute,' the man said abruptly, 'Miss whatever your name is, your pump was taking water from my dam free, gratis and for nothing. Now I don't care what kind of an arrangement you had with the previous owners, but I'm not running some kind of a charitable institution, and as for me coming to see *you*, I should have thought it ought to be the other way round. You've used my water for a month now. Did you expect it to continue without any kind of representation on your part?'

'I did,' Camira said through clenched teeth, 'try to see you. Several times. As a matter of fact I haunted this place. But this is only the second time you've been here since you bought the place, may I remind you, and I missed you the other time. I even wrote to you care of your solicitor. *You* didn't have the courtesy to reply!'

'Because I didn't get the letter,' he said tersely.

'But you must have,' Camira objected. 'I got the name and address from Mrs Thompson. Are you trying to tell me I'm lying? Why, I,' her voice rose, 'I could hit you for that!' She stepped forward fully prepared in the heat of the moment to carry out her threat, but the man had other ideas and she found both her wrists suddenly clamped in an iron grasp.

'Let me . . . *go*!' she spat at him. She stopped short at the look of smothered laughter on his face. 'Oh, you're impossible!' she stormed.

The laughter subsided and he said evenly, 'No, you are, Miss Fire-Eater. Tell me, do you make a habit of barging into people's houses at this ungodly hour and offering to beat them up?'

'Only insufferable, pigheaded. . . .'

'That's enough,' he said coldly, and his grip bit cruelly into her wrists. He looked past her to the boy who was standing behind them still open-mouthed. 'Put some coffee on, will you, Tim. And you,' he said to Camira, 'if you don't want to say goodbye to every last drop of water on the Lodge, will sit down in there,' he gestured to an open doorway which led to a room equipped as an office, 'and we'll sort this out once and for all. In a civilised manner.' He emphasised his words and let go of her wrists.

Camira rubbed them involuntarily, and stopped as soon as she realised what she was doing. She opened her mouth to say proudly that she didn't want his water or his coffee, but her own eyes widened as a movement beyond him caught her eye and she felt her own jaw sag before she shut it with an almost audible click.

For a girl had appeared in the passageway behind Marcus Riley, the most beautiful girl Camira had ever seen for all, or possibly aided by the fact that she had nothing on but a luxurious coffee-coloured satin sheet clutched around her.

She shut her eyes and opened them just as quickly. The girl was still there, her rosy lips formed into a little pout and her magnificent tawny hair streaming across her bare shoulders.

Marcus Riley said, 'Tim, what are you waiting for?' But he turned as a sudden look of burning embarrassment crossed the lad's face and he pushed past Camira with a muttered apology.

'Marc,' the girl drawled languidly as his eyes fell on her and she moved slowly aside to let Tim pass, 'what's going on? Such a row, and it's so early.' She pouted prettily again. 'You told me it was very peaceful around here,' she said with gentle reproach. 'Who is this . . . person?' She raised one ivory arm in Camira's direction and Camira found herself holding her breath in case the sheet slipped. But it didn't, and for some insane reason Camira found herself wanting to laugh. She has a way with sheets, the lady, she thought ironically. If I tried to do that. . . .

She glanced at Marcus Riley and was arrested to see a nerve throb once in his jaw. His eyes were not on the vision of loveliness standing before him but on the kitchen doorway through which Tim had disappeared. He said, 'You shouldn't get around like that, Lisa. There are other people living in this house. Not to mention the unexpected visitors we get,' he added sardonically.

The girl looked stricken. 'I'm sorry, Marc,' she said huskily. 'I won't do it again.' She glanced at Camira from beneath her long dark lashes and then looked around quickly as if to make sure Tim had not rejoined them. Her stricken look changed to one of sparkling eagerness and she touched Marc Riley's forearm lightly with one beautifully manicured hand as she smiled up into his eyes. 'Don't be cross with me, Marc. If you come back to bed I'll make it up to you,' she promised in an audible undertone.

Audible to Camira anyway, although it possibly wouldn't have penetrated to the kitchen where Tim could be heard moving around.

Camira blushed and stood rooted to the spot, wishing the floor would open up beneath her feet. She cleared her throat and said, 'Excuse me, I'll go now. . . .'

'What a good idea!' the girl said with such an air of false ingenuity that Camira was suddenly possessed of an incredible desire to slap her face. She turned stiffly, however, but not before she saw the open amusement on Marcus Riley's face and she knew he'd read her acute embarrassment accurately and was enjoying it.

He said to her, '*You'll* go into the office, mate. And you, Lisa, will get some clothes on and do something about breakfast—that is, if you want to go for that ride I promised you.' He turned back to Camira. 'After you, Miss . . . what is your name, by the way?'

Camira's first thought was one of resistance, but his hand on her arm somehow seemed to preclude this, so she marched into the room with her head held high and blushed again as she heard him say over his shoulder to the girl still standing in the passageway, 'This shouldn't take long, honey. If you're a good girl, I'll let you ride the new filly.' He shut the door and indicated a chair for Camira to sit on. She sank down into it. He said, as he leant his shoulders back against the door, 'I think it's about time you told me your name at least.'

'It's Johnston,' she said gruffly.

'Miss . . . Johnston?' he queried as his eyes sought her left hand.

'Yes,' she said distinctly.

'Ah.' He pushed himself away from the door and sat down opposite the desk to her.

'What does that mean?' Camira enquired icily.

'I'm not sure,' he said with a quirk to his lips. 'But it could explain your extreme discomfort.' His hazel eyes explored her still warm cheeks. 'You know,' he said on a gentle note of satire, 'if you insist on making these headlong dashes into people's private lives, you're bound to come up against . . . something like this. I'm surprised it hasn't happened to you before.'

Camira took a deep breath. 'You talk as if I make a habit of this,' she said contemptuously. 'I can assure you I don't. However, I did feel extremely . . . provoked. But before I get on to that subject,' she said fierily, 'you mentioned people's private lives. I'm surprised to find you feel so strongly about it. Really I am. Because you don't seem to mind parading your . . . lady loves in a state of undress to say the least, and in very obvious circumstances, before an impressionable teenage boy—or perhaps you're hoping to have him follow in your footsteps. At an early age,' she added sweetly.

His face went pale with anger and for a moment Camira bitterly regretted what she'd said and felt a shaft of fear shoot through her. He looks as if he could murder me, she thought incoherently.

'Miss Johnston,' he said evenly through thinned lips, 'may I give you some advice? You've tried my patience almost to the limit this morning. Your last remarks particularly. Tim is my half-brother, and I don't need any help from anyone, least of all yourself, as to how I should organise our lives. And so far as your water goes. . . .

Water! The word seemed to pound its way into Camira's brain, and she winced and closed her eyes suddenly and the rest of his speech flowed above her head, unheard and unheeded.

What a fool you are, Camira Johnston, she told herself. What a blind, stupid idiot! His water means more to you than anything else in the world, and yet ever since you saw those uprooted pipes this morning you've done your level best to ensure you never get another drop of it. You've indulged in a temper tantrum, unequalled for years, you've stuck your nose into his affairs and made insulting remarks. You've. . . .

She bowed her head, conscious now of a sick feeling at the pit of her stomach; also suddenly conscious that the room was quite silent. She clenched her hands together painfully and stood up abruptly. There was nothing she could do to rectify matters.

She said stiffly, 'I'm . . . I'll go now. Good day.' She avoided his eyes and turned to the door.

'You'll go nowhere, Miss Johnston, until I say so. Sit down,' he said sharply.

She turned back but didn't look at him. 'Please . . . I'm *sorry*. I haven't acted very well. I think it's better if I just . . . leave.'

She turned away again, but he was up in a flash and he

came round the desk like some big lithe cat. Before she guessed what he was about he'd picked her up in an extremely undignified fireman's hold and then as she gasped for breath he dumped her unceremoniously down into the chair she'd just vacated. She shot up, but his hand came down heavily on her shoulder and she sat down equally heavily once more. She looked up and their eyes locked. The browny-green depths of his seemed to mock her cool-looking grey ones.

'I don't think, Miss Johnston,' he said deliberately, 'that you're any match for me, but I'm quite willing to continue this little contest if you want to.'

She licked her lips. 'I . . . there's nothing more to be said,' she whispered shakily.

He lifted his hand from her shoulder and bent to retrieve her straw hat from the floor. 'You must have a short very memory, then,' he said wryly. He handed her the hat. 'Your . . . hat, ma'am,' he said quizzically, and walked round the desk. 'Forgive me if I was wrong, but I got the distinct impression you originally came to discuss water with me. Before you got . . . er . . . sidetracked, that is.'

Her eyes flew to his face and she swallowed. But his expression gave her no clue as to what he had in mind. He's only playing with me now, she thought. Retaliating for the things I said. Taunting me. . . .

She said quietly, 'I did come to discuss water. And I did make every effort to contact you about it before this. Un—unfortunately I . . . I'm rather awkwardly placed at the moment. I couldn't afford to . . . pay you for it. I did have a proposition to put to you instead, but now . . . well, it doesn't seem quite as feasible as it did,' she said with a rush.

'No?' he drawled with a sardonic inflection. 'Why don't

you let me be the judge of that?'

'No,' she said slowly, nettled afresh by his tone.

'Don't let Lisa put you off,' he drawled. 'She's not here permanently.'

Camira jerked upright as the full import of his words sank in. 'You mean . . . you thought . . . how dare you!' she said incredulously.

'Why not?' He shrugged. 'You've just told me you don't have any money. And from what I've seen of your place there's nothing else there I could use.' He grinned at her outraged expression. 'It's one of the oldest forms of barter, you know. Why should you, particularly, be so above it?'

'Because I am,' she said fiercely. 'It never entered my head. I . . . I . . . .'

'Perhaps you should let it, Miss Johnston.' His eyes roamed over her in a way that brought another blush to her cheeks. 'With a bit of effort you might not be bad-looking, you know. Everything seems to be there in the right proportion—so far as one can tell under those . . . clothes. You might even find it has a beneficial effect on you. It might make you less irascible. I'm told,' he murmured, 'spinsters do get that way.'

Camira stared at him, totally bereft of words, and it was perhaps fortunate for her, as her fists clenched and unclenched, that the door swung open at that moment and Tim's freckled face appeared round it.

'Brought your coffee,' he said. 'Still want it?'

'Sure do, Tim,' said Marcus Riley. 'Thanks.'

Tim put a small wooden tray down on the desk. He glanced at Camira, but she was staring down at her hands. He said, 'Er . . . breakfast, if you can call it that, is a-comin' up. Shall we keep yours hot, Marc?'

Marc grimaced slightly and he and his little brother

exchanged a sudden grin. 'I won't be long now, Tim.'

'Okay!' Tim retreated and closed the door behind him, but not before he had cast Camira another speculative glance which she didn't see.

'Your coffee, Miss Johnston,' Marcus Riley said. 'It should be drinkable even if breakfast is not quite edible. Still, I suppose it's too much to ask for all that beauty to be interested in cooking. Are you a good cook, Miss Johnston?'

'Yes. No!' Camira said disjointedly. 'Look, will you just let me out of here? You've had your fun at my expense. We're square now. Let's just leave it be.'

He didn't say anything for a time but stared at her intently until she dropped her eyes. Then he said, 'That still leaves you with no water, I gather. How will you cope?'

'I won't die of thirst,' she said evenly. 'I have a rainwater tank for my . . . personal needs. For the rest, I'll manage somehow.'

His eyes narrowed. 'Why is this water so important to you? And what arrangement—I gather you must have had some arrangement—did you have with the previous owners?'

She said wearily, 'I thought Mrs Thompson *must* have mentioned it to you. I . . . I didn't realise you knew nothing about it.'

He said equably, 'The first I knew of it was yesterday afternoon when I discovered the pump on the far end of the dam going hell for leather. It didn't take much to realise where the pipes ended up and I honestly couldn't see any reason at the time why I should provide a free watering service for the district. And I only met Mrs Thompson on one occasion, you know. During which she was still understandably upset about the thought of parting with her beloved property so close to the death of her husband.

Strangely, her main concern was her dog. As you see, I took him over.'

Camira winced. 'Yes,' she said slowly, 'I see now. She had so much on her mind.' She looked up. 'But my letter. I did honestly write to your solicitor.'

'It's probably still sitting in his office. I've been in New Zealand for a couple of weeks at the yearling sales. You'd better tell me all about it.'

Camira hesitated and moistened her lips. How can I tell ... *this* man? she thought wildly. It sounds so ... silly. Especially after what he's said.

An impatient drumming sound on the desk brought her back with a start. All right! she told herself. But if he laughs or makes any more improper suggestions, he'd better just watch out!

'I have a vegetable garden, at the weekends, mainly, there's a lot of traffic on this road because the area is a very popular launching spot for people with small boats and the bar at Jumpinpin is a great fishing ground. I sell my vegetables and fruit from a little stall I have on the roadside, together with other odds and ends.'

'Like what?' he interrupted.

'Well, pottery, weaving, macramé work and pot-plants. But,' her voice faltered for the first time, 'the vegetables are undoubtedly my best seller. The sandy soil in this area is rather fertile and it doesn't only produce sugar-cane. You can grow tomatoes and strawberries and—well, provided that is. ...'

'Provided you have water. I take it you don't have a dam on your acreage or the means to put one in?'

'I did. ...' She stopped and shook her head. 'I don't, you're right. But I hope to be able to, in the not so far distant future—if I can keep going,' she said levelly.

'I see.'

I doubt if you do, Camira thought bitterly.

'And just how did you repay the Thompsons' for the water you drew off the Lodge?'

She gritted her teeth. 'I . . . supplied them with fresh vegetables, I . . . cleared their manure and I,' she took a deep breath, 'I was their housekeeper. In a way. I . . . came in for two days a week and cleaned up for them. Mrs Thompson was getting on, you see, and it's a big house. . . .' Her voice trailed away helplessly as his face came alive with amusement.

'Do you mean to tell me you were going to offer your services as a housekeeper to me?' He laughed openly with a flash of white teeth. 'Perhaps I wasn't so far off target after all,' he murmured.

Camira said furiously, 'I'd no more dream of being your housekeeper than . . . than. . . .'

'Taking a trip to Sodom and Gomorrah?' he finished for her, and laughed even harder. 'Dear me,' he said finally, 'this has turned out to be a fun morning after all. Don't look so pained, Miss Johnston. As a matter of fact I have a perfectly respectable housekeeper arriving tomorrow, so the post is not open.'

'Well, that settles the matter, doesn't it,' Camira said bitterly. 'And now that you've finished laughing, may I leave? Because if you think I'm going to get down on my knees and beg you for this water, you're totally wrong.'

He sobered. 'You could try,' he said. 'Unfortunately I'm not a very philanthropic person. And water,' he added, 'is a rather valuable resource in this area.'

'I'm aware of that,' Camira bit out.

He grinned. 'Of course.' He put his head on one side and regarded her quizzically, 'Tell me,' he said, 'talking of resources, you seem to be a rather resourceful person your-self, or rather a jack of all trades, anyway. Can you think of anything you *could* do here in exchange for this water? Other than housekeeping?'

Camira bit her lip. 'I. . . .' she started to say, but stopped. I don't want to work for him, she reminded herself. I don't ever want to have to see him again. Oh God, what an impossible situation!

'Go on,' he said keenly.

'I . . . you mentioned yearlings. I'm . . . I've had a lot of experience with horses, especially yearlings. Helping to break them in and so on,' she ended lamely.

'I suppose I should be surprised,' he commented, 'but I'm not. As it happens all our yearlings are broken in by the time they arrive here. They are—they *will* be ready to go straight into training. However, I do have a team of horses arriving any day now, all seasoned gallopers, and it so happens I was thinking of employing some local help. How does the position of a strapper sound to you, Miss Johnston? On a trial basis for, let's say, one month? In return for the use of my dam? Would it interfere with your gardening? Or your weaving or potting?'

But Camira was for once immune to his sarcasm. As a matter of fact his offer had almost taken her breath away. To work with horses again—to have the life-sustaining water turned on. It was like an impossible dream come true.

She said breathlessly, 'Are you serious? You're not —teasing me?'

Marcus Riley tightened his lips. 'You really don't have much of an opinion of me, do you? No, I'm not teasing you, but I promise you I'm a hard taskmaster and if you don't come up to scratch, you'll be out on your ear. And all the water will stay on this side of the fence.'

Camira swallowed at his curt tone and could think of nothing to say. 'When do I start?' she asked finally.

'Tomorrow morning at sun-up. Don't be late.' He pulled out a desk drawer and withdrew a book and a pen. 'What's your first name, by the way? Miss Johnston is a hell of mouthful. You'll find we're quite informal at Camira Lodge.'

She rose from her chair. 'I won't be late,' she promised. 'And my name is—Camira.'

And as she turned to go she knew that for the first time since she'd met Marcus Riley, she'd succeeding in jolting him.

CHAPTER TWO

IT was a week later that Camira stood on her doorstep and took one last lingering look around her small property as the sun set in a sea of molten gold and deepening blue. She had just finished watering her vegetables and the well dug beds gleamed as the last rays of the sun alighted briefly on scattered droplets of moisture and the rich tang of damp earth assailed her nostrils. At the far end of the small paddock that she hoped one day would accommodate a horse of her own, two tall gum trees stood sentinel, their trunks stark and white but their leaves touched with the almost living rose-colour of the sun. And beyond, the drab olive of the mangroves stretched unbroken towards the coast.

She turned and looked thoughtfully at the riot of bougainvillea and Golden Shower that threatened almost to smother the verandah end of her cottage. I'll have to trim it soon, she thought. The cottage was not much more than a log cabin, but it was sturdy and quite adequate for two people and even had a rustic charm of its own. Although now, of course, there was only one. . . .

She shook herself resolutely. No good thinking those thoughts, and she shut the screen door firmly behind her. A shower and a meal in that order are what you need, Camira, and then a leisurely evening spent reading that new book Jane Sinclair brought over today . . . all night if you like, because it's Sunday tomorrow and the only day of the week that you don't have to get up at the crack of dawn. Not that Sunday could actually be termed a rest day, she told herself amusedly. In fact, so far as her stall went it was her busiest day, but an extra stint today had ensured that everything was ready.

As she stood under the shower her mind roamed back over the past incredible week. Every morning before sun-up she'd set out across the paddock and climbed the fence to Camira Lodge and spent the next four hours doing possibly what she enjoyed best in the world. And before her eyes, so to speak, she had watched The Lodge come alive again. Twelve thoroughbreds had arrived, and as in the best racing stables, they were treated like prima donnas. Camira worked steadily each day, washing horses, walking horses, swimming horses, bedding their stalls and feeding them.

The only thing I haven't done, she thought wryly, is ride them. But still, I'm not complaining. It's been enough.

Neither have I seen much of Marcus Riley, she thought as she turned the water off and reached for a towel. And I'm certainly not complaining about that either. A peculiar sensation prickled her bare skin as a vision of her new employer rose to mind. I could really die of embarrassment, she thought. I must have been mad to behave like that on that first morning. The things he said! But no, she told herself sternly, I really didn't deserve all of his comments.

All the same, as if prompted by some inner volition she hung up the towel carefully and regarded her naked image in the long bathroom mirror. I might not be petite and dainty and absolutely exquisite, she thought ruefully, but I'm not unfeminine, am I? She looked at herself critically. Or am I? David certainly seemed to think I was quite feminine. Or did he really? He certainly seemed to have a lot of trouble keeping his hands off me. Until, that is, he discovered how destitute I was.

Her eyes hardened as she took in the long slender sweep of her legs, the rounded curve of her hips, her flat stomach and small waist and her generous, well-shaped breasts. But it wasn't enough for David, was it? she reminded herself. And no doubt it wouldn't prove much of an enticement for Marcus Riley, accustomed as he obviously was to the very epitome . . . what am I thinking? she asked herself with a sudden wry grin. As if I care two hoots for what he's accustomed to!

Then why, an unkind inner voice prompted, did that Lisa girl make you feel like a gangling overgrown colt? And about as unfragile?

'I wonder?' she said out aloud, her grey eyes suddenly pensive. 'Perhaps she has that effect on most women. And after all, some would say he's a most attractive man. Those,' she added, 'who could detach his physical presence from his personality or who had not had the misfortune to cross swords with him.' She shrugged and laughed at her own reflection and walked through to her bedroom to get dressed.

Although her most frequent attire was either jeans or shorts and a shirt, she had made it a habit after a long tiring day to change into something long, cool and loose, and tonight she picked out a feather-light dress of a plain hyacinth blue that fell in loose folds from a narrow band that formed the neckline to the floor. The blue she knew did something for her eyes and she thought of her mother suddenly who had often said to her that she was lucky to have inherited her father's grey eyes because they seemed to change colour with what she wore. She inspected the dress and removed a thread from the hemline, then hesitated for a moment, her hand outstretched to gather up a bra from the open drawer of her duchess. But she dropped the bra back and removed only a pair of panties which she donned before pulling the blue dress over her head.

'It's not as if anyone's going to see me,' she murmured to herself, 'and in any case, it doesn't fit tightly anywhere. Besides, no one seems to wear bras much at all these days. Only the straightlaced, prim, *spinsterish* Camira Johnston. Damn!' she added forcefully. 'Damn . . . him, damn David, damn all men. Except one, and even he had to die and leave me alone.'

She marched into the kitchen dashing angrily at the tears on her cheeks. 'I'm going to make myself a delicious supper, then I'll put on my favourite music and relax! And they can all go to the devil.'

Several hours later she was doing just that, engrossed in her new book and with the haunting strains of the Moonlight Sonata floating through the air.

For some reason Camira could never explain, she pre-

ferred to do her reading sitting on the floor, and she sat
there now with one knee drawn up, the other leg curled
beneath her bending forward slightly with her long fair hair
which she had left loose after her shower looped behind her
ears and the tip of her tongue protruding slightly as her eyes
skimmed the page.

She could never afterwards say what it was that alerted
her. She certainly hadn't heard a car, but she looked up
now, suddenly uneasy. The single lighted lamp was beside
her on a small table, bathing her in its warm glow, but the
rest of the room, although not large, was dim and shadowy.
She looked around warily and then a sudden sound drew her
attention to the screen door that led to the verandah.
Immediately her heart began to beat with thick, heavy
strokes. It was hard to see beyond the circle of light, but
she was positive there was a man standing out there. She
tensed violently as she remembered it wasn't even locked.
An old maxim of her grandfather's flashed into her mind
from nowhere: he who hesitates is lost . . . in this case *she*,
she thought fiercely, but then in this case, whoever is out
there might have taken on more than they can handle. And
in a single fluid motion she was on her feet with the heavy
pottery-based lamp in her hand. One swift tug pulled the
cord from the wall and she flew across the room with every
intention of delivering a solid blow to the head of the
intruder as she heard the squeak of the screen-door opening. . . .

What followed was something Camira doubted she
would ever forget. The intruder must have realised her
intentions, because he certainly set about to deal with them
most promptly. The lamp was wrested from her grasp and
she found herself grabbed painfully and clamped to the
man's broad chest so that she found it difficult to breathe.

Still she fought him with all the strength she could muster, but her resistance was puny, she knew, as she pummelled at him with her fists and tried to kick him with her bare feet.

'Will you stop it!' she panted. 'I'll. . . .'

'Stop what?' an amused voice drawled into her ear. '*You're* doing all the fighting. I'm merely protecting myself.'

She froze. She knew that voice and several variations of it. Sardonic, curt and businesslike, loverlike. . . .

'That's better,' he commented dryly, and withdrew his arm.

Camira swayed where she stood, as much from the abrupt release as the realisation of who her captor had been. Several moments later the yellow glow of the lamp flooded on and she stood there blinking up at him.

He said, 'You're a regular wildcat, Miss Camira Johnston, aren't you? Tell me, is there something about me of which I'm unaware, that triggers off this insatiable desire you seem to have to attack me?'

She stared into his hazel eyes so amused and mocking. 'You!' she gasped.

'Yes, me. Marc Riley.' He put a finger on her chin. 'You could have laid me out with that lamp, you know.'

Her cheeks burned. She said stiffly, 'I'm sorry,' then felt a wave of anger course through her. 'But why didn't you say something? I didn't know who was out there. It could have been . . . anyone!' she finished hotly.

'Indeed it could,' he agreed. 'And although I know you think I'm the devil's representative himself, I really didn't come here with thoughts of pillage and rape on my mind. Quite the opposite, in fact.' He grinned whitely as she flushed again. 'The point I'm trying to make is, though, you just don't seem to realise you're no match for a fully-grown man and you don't seem to take any precautions despite the fact that you live here alone. Don't you think that's rather unwise?'

'I haven't had any problems up to now. Not everyone goes around with thoughts of seduction continually on their mind, you know,' she said tartly.

He threw back his head and laughed. 'You . . . you know what you remind me of?' he said at last.

Camira drew herself to her full height, furiously. 'No! And I don't—and I don't want to.'

'Very well,' he said with a sudden grim look in his eyes. 'But you can't stop me telling you this. You're crazy living here on your own with not even a dog to protect you. But at least, if you make a habit of sitting around half undressed in the lamplight, lock the doors, will you, because whether you want to believe it or not, my dear innocent, women do get bashed and raped and often with far less provocation than you offered.'

Her eyes flew from his lean, angry face to the lamp, to the spot on the carpet where she had sat, to the screen door.

'Yes,' he said with a controlled irony, 'the lamp behind you made that flimsy garment about as transparent as a sheet of glass.'

She closed her eyes and with a reflex action crossed her arms over her body, but at his soft chuckle her eyes flew open and she blinked to see that he had sprawled down in one of her armchairs and was studying her with amused derision. 'It's a bit late for that, isn't it?' he said softly.

Camira bit her lip. A torrent of angry cutting remarks sprang to mind, but something stronger held her back. A warning light seemed to flash and she surprised even herself as she said with a semblance of calm she was far from feeling, 'I suppose it is a bit late. I get so few visitors, you see, I didn't think, and anyway I generally hear them arrive.' She turned towards her bedroom. 'If you'll excuse me, I'll put something more suitable on.'

But when she returned, clad once again in jeans and a shirt, he looked her up and down and grimaced visibly. 'Very suitable,' he murmured, but she saw a muscle move in his cheek and knew he was laughing at her.

Oh no! You're not going to provoke me again, Mr Riley, she told herself grimly. Ever again. She said politely, 'Would you like a cup of coffee? And perhaps you'd like to tell me what you came to see me about?' She couldn't prevent, however, a tiny edge creeping into her voice as she added, 'And how you managed to arrive so silently?'

He stood up lazily. 'Thanks, a cup of coffee wouldn't go amiss. And I copied your usual mode of perambulation between our two properties, I climbed the fence and walked. It's a beautiful night.'

As he spoke he had walked towards her, she realised as she stood at the sink and filled the kettle. For some strange reason the knowledge that he was standing right behind her now made her heart beat a little faster.

But she said lightly, 'I'm surprised you didn't get eaten alive. The mosquitoes and sandflies are very active at this time of night.' She turned and found her head was level with his chin, and found also that he appeared to have no intention of moving out of her way.

She said pointedly, 'Excuse me. Why don't you sit down? This won't take a minute and I've . . . I've got some fresh apple strudel to go with it.' She tilted her head back and glanced at him, a glance that wasn't quite in keeping with polite remarks.

That same muscle quivered in his cheek again and she knew instinctively that he was perfectly aware of her increased heart rate. Just don't you blush, Camira, she warned herself fiercely. He can taunt you all he likes, but if he gets no reaction he'll soon tire of it.

But he moved away lightly and said casually, 'Apple strudel? And by the look of it,' he pointed to loaf tins standing on the counter, their contents neatly covered with a clean tea-towel, 'homemade bread? Are you the same girl who a week ago couldn't make up her mind whether she was a good cook or not?' he asked humourously.

Camira grinned reluctantly and said honestly, 'I'm a new hand at bread, actually. I've had my fair share of failures. There's a definite knack to it.'

'What beats me,' he said as he took the cup of coffee she handed him, 'is how you find the time for all these pursuits.'

She flinched inwardly as they sat down and she placed the apple strudel between them. It wasn't a question so much of finding the time but filling it. She said easily, though, 'Oh, I have plenty of time. I live a very quiet life, you see.'

His eyes narrowed slightly as they rested on her downcast face. 'I do see,' he murmured, and a slight frown touched his brow. 'But I find it a bit strange,' he admitted. 'Most girls of your age would probably die of boredom. What is your age, by the way?'

'Twenty-one,' she said, and couldn't resist adding with with a small grin, 'definitely old enough to be classified as a spinster.'

He grinned back, and her stupid heart, which seemed to have acquired a new life of its own tonight, raced suddenly.

'Touché,' he said softly. 'I suppose I did ask for that.'

Camira deliberately made herself look blank.

It seemed he didn't appreciate this, though, because he moved his shoulders restlessly and said, 'No, don't look like that. I was just beginning to think you were human after all.

Tell me, did they name you after Camira Lodge or it after you?'

She tensed and then forced herself to relax. 'You know,' she said not as a question but a statement of fact.

'Some of it,' he admitted. 'It's not difficult to get the locals talking and I've met a few of them this last week. Was that one of the reasons why you were in such a magnificent rage when we first met?' He grinned reminiscently.

Camira fiddled with a piece of apple strudel absently, wishing she could deny it. Wishing it, and at the same time feeling quite angry that he of all people should be so acute. But honesty was a habit with her, even if it was slightly belated in this case.

'I . . . I think it was,' she said quietly. She forced herself to smile. 'But really, I've got over it. It's only the odd occasion that it gets to me.' She hesitated and then said brightly, 'As for the name, my grandfather was born in a tiny town, more of a dot on the map really, called Camira Creek. He was rather sentimental about it.'

'I take it,' said Marc Riley after a moment, 'that your grandfather was responsible for Camira Lodge in its heyday? It was a very famous training establishment, wasn't it? What went wrong?'

Camira took a breath. 'My grandfather and my father made it what it was. But horses are always something of a gamble, and . . . things went wrong. They, mistakenly as it turned out, went into the breeding side, but this isn't good country for *breeding* horses. I doubt if these types of coastal plains ever are, and to add to it the stallion they purchased turned out to be an expensive flop.' She shrugged. 'It can happen to anyone. Anyway, finally there was no option but to sell the place. Most of it,' she amended, 'apart from this little corner.' She glanced around. 'As a matter of fact this is the first house that was ever built on Camira. My grandfather built it himself and brought my grandmother here as a bride.'

He sipped his coffee and studied her intently. He said, 'How old were you when it was sold? First sold?'

'Eighteen.'

'And you've lived here ever since? Surely it would have been easier to have made a clean break?'

'Sometimes I'm sure it would have,' she said wryly. 'Other times . . . well . . . But I couldn't, you see. My parents were killed in a light plane crash round about the same time, but my grandfather was still alive and he was . . . just devastated. He'd lived here all his adult life, you see, my grandmother's buried here, and I knew that to uproot him completely after all that happened would kill him. The sale hadn't been quite finalised when my parents died, so I went to Mr Thompson and managed to negotiate with him to have this corner subdivided from the rest of the property. And—well, that's how I come to be here. I think . . . I think he was happy and at peace for the two years he had left to him, my grandfather. He always said some of the happiest times of his life were spent right here in this little cottage.'

Marc Riley sat back and pushed his hands into his pockets. His expression was unfathomable to Camira as she looked at him, looked at the lids of his downcast eyes with their absurdly long dark lashes.

Then his lids swept up and she glanced away in sudden confusion and thought, Dear God, I hope he doesn't think I've been playing on his sympathy! Those are *some* of the facts, anyway. And he did ask, point-blank.

But he said on an almost rough note, 'How come you have to grow vegetables for a living, then? I know what I paid for Camira Lodge and it wasn't an insignificant amount.

Surely you didn't give it away to the Thompsons?'

'No,' she said evenly, 'but it was heavily mortgaged. And after we'd, in effect, bought back this part, there was very little left.' How little you'll never know, she added, but beneath her breath.

They stared at each other across the table and she was conscious of a sudden peculiar tension in the air as her cool grey eyes clashed with his. It was as if he was angry about something.

He said abruptly, 'Well, how come you're still living on the smell of an oil rag, grovelling in the dirt when you're not housekeeping for other people in your ancestral home? Why don't you get out and start to live again, like any normal girl? You seem to be reasonably intelligent. Get yourself a decent, well-paid job. If your grandfather's dead now, you don't have to languish here for ever,' he added contemptuously.

Camira gasped and all her previous wariness deserted her as if it had never existed. Her eyes blazed as she said furiously, 'You might think it's a contemptible occupation growing food, Mr Riley, but I happen to enjoy it. Crazy as it may sound to you, it gives me quite a sense of satisfaction to be self-sufficient, not to have to be dependent on anything but my own two hands. . . .'

'And my water,' he shot in. Which was unfortunately the last drop of fuel to the flame as far as Camira was concerned.

'What's so wrong with that?' she spat at him: 'I'm paying for it. And if you're not happy with the job I'm doing, you have only to say the word. If you think my whole world depends on you, think again, mate! I've met plenty of obstacles that seemed insurmountable before, but I've always found a way through them, and I will again. And while we're on the subject, just what is a 'normal girl' to you? Is it someone who has nothing but thoughts of men and clothes and money and having a good time at all costs yet is quite incapable of coming to grips with the bare facts of life!' She paused and drew a breath. 'You might be able to fill your bed with them,' she said fiercely, 'but we're not all like that, believe me. And anyway,' she added ironically, 'they say like attracts like. . . .'

Her voice trailed off as she saw the white flash of his teeth, startling against his tan. He was laughing silently, and she ground her teeth in bitter, futile rage.

'Wow!' he said finally, still on a note of laughter. 'You don't pull any punches, do you? Don't stop, Camira. Go on and tell me exactly what you think of me. You were trying, I gather, to tell me that such a dissolute person as myself, so lacking in any moral fibre, could never attract the devotion, wholehearted devotion, of someone, say, like yourself?'

'No!' she said confusedly, and thought wildly, I didn't mean to sound so pompous, but he has a habit . . . making me. And a spurt of fresh anger flooded her. I might as well be in for a pound as a penny.

'Yes,' she said coldly, 'the likes of you could never attract me in a million light years.'

He'd been lounging back enjoying her discomfort, but at her last words he straightened and leant towards her across the table. 'Oho,' he said softly and still with that hateful note of amusement, 'it might not have been very wise to throw down that particular gauntlet, Camira. Who's to say I won't pick it up?'

'You . . . wouldn't! *You couldn't*,' she said scornfully, her cheeks burning brightly and her breast heaving from sheer suppressed rage. Or was it? she wondered fleetingly.

'I mightn't,' he agreed. 'I think you're rather brave to

assume so categorically that I couldn't, however.' And he let his eyes roam over her in a manner that left her in no doubt he was mentally undressing her.

'Oh!' she breathed. 'I *hate* you! You've got to be the most conceited. . . .' She stopped and her eyes widened as Marc stood up lithely and she grabbed the arms of her chair to stop herself from being hauled out of it, but his lean, strong fingers prised hers apart and he hauled her upright so that she stood facing him with her wrists imprisoned in his hands.

'Do you now?' he said barely audibly, and she felt his warm breath fan her forehead. He transferred her wrists to one hand and with the other under her chin, forced her to look up at him. 'You're very, very sure of yourself, Camira.' He traced the outline of her jaw with one finger. 'You seem to think you're above the rest of us poor mortals. Certainly, in this respect. But I honestly don't altogether believe it, my dear.'

She stood as if transfixed as his wandering finger explored with the lightest touch behind one ear and then, still with a touch like silk, he trailed his fingers down the slender column of her neck and although she guessed, fearfully, what was coming, with her wrists still clamped in a vicelike grip, she was powerless to resist.

The top buttons of her shirt gave way at a flick and those long, powerful fingers were equally adept with the front fastening of the bra she now wore. She tensed as the clasp gave way and for a moment her eyes rested imploringly on his.

'Relax,' he murmured. 'I'm not going to hurt you.'

But that he was as good as his word was no consolation to Camira. She backed away determinedly and found she was jammed in a corner. And all the time his fingers roamed delicately over her now exposed breasts and she felt as if she was drowning in his dark, intent look, drowning in a flood of erotic sensation. But the bitterest blow was the sudden look of triumph in his eyes as, despite herself, her nipples hardened and stood erect like rosy peaks beneath his fingers.

Suddenly she was free and, with a grave look that she knew masked hidden laughter, Marc reclosed the clasp of her bra and did up the buttons of her shirt.

'There,' he said with gentle mockery and his knuckles still resting with a burning touch in the hollows at the base of her throat, 'you can hate me as much as you like, Camira, but you'd be silly to try and pretend you're not human like the rest of us. *That*'s a bare, simple fact of life and I think I just proved it,' He grinned devilishly. 'I'm quite willing to go on proving it too, should you still have doubts.'

He turned to go, but turned back almost immediately and pulled something from his shirt pocket. 'I almost forgot.' He looked at the object in his hand and shook his head. He said wryly, 'For a girl with such definite opinions about me, your choice of notepaper for communications of a business nature to me, is odd, to say the least.'

Camira stared. It was the letter she had written to him care of his solicitor he held and was now sniffing.

'It's scented too. As if the violets and roses weren't enough.' He smiled faintly. 'I'm afraid my solicitor is rather a stuffy old gentleman and he gets quite irate about— as he puts it—having his address used for my fan-mail. His words I quote. It was returned to me unopened with some papers that arrived today.'

'But I. . . .' she stammered.

Marc interjected swiftly, 'Oh, I've read it now. Very proper and correct it is too. But somehow flowered, scented notepaper seems to carry its own implication, doesn't it?' he said with an enigmatic glance.

Camira licked her lips and stared at the pale pink envelope now lying on the table. I knew that was a mistake, she told herself desolately. And with a calmness born of despair possibly, she didn't allow the tears that were threatening to fall, and she didn't sink into a chair because her legs felt unaccountably weak.

And when he said from the doorway, 'So I'll see you Monday morning, Camira?' she nodded after only a small struggle with herself and didn't lift the heavy dictionary off the bookshelf beside her and throw it at him. But his low laugh after he had let himself out and she heard his footsteps going down the stairs achieved what his words had not, and she did all those things plus a few more.

It wasn't until her rage had blown itself out and she was sitting at the table with her head in her hands that the most unwelcome, distasteful thought occurred to her. Was this orgy of anger directed as much at herself as him?

CHAPTER THREE

AT sunset the following day, Camira closed her stall and with an aching back but a feeling of satisfaction walked slowly up the winding rutted drive to the cottage. It had been a very good day. She'd sold every vegetable and every piece of fruit on display and more besides, as well as some of her handiwork.

She unlocked her door wearily and with a relieved sigh sank down into a chair at the dining room table. It was the first chance she'd had to sit down all day, but she thought, as she emptied a calico bag of money on the table, it must have been worth it. A perfect day weather-wise plus the knowledge that the bream were biting off Jumpinpin had seen a steady stream of cars and boats pass and an equally steady proportion of them stop at the stall.

'Phew!' She stared at the money in front of her and reached behind her and withdrew four large screw-top bottles from a cupboard. Camira's accounting system was simple but effective. Each bottle bore a label, Rates and Electricity, Dam, Housekeeping, and Horse. She opened the bottles and began sorting the money into piles. Several times she paused indecisively with her hand hovering over the pile that would go into the bottle marked Horse and then reluctantly passed it by. Consequently this pile, together with Housekeeping, was a lot smaller than the other two. Once she stopped counting and sorting and stared in front of her unseeingly for a long moment, and then with a slight grimace she scooped up the money set aside for a horse and placed it on the 'Dam' pile.

'If I keep going like this,' she told herself as she emptied the 'Horse' bottle into the 'Dam' bottle and put it away out of sight in the cupboard with a quick movement, 'I'll have that dam, or at least a bore, and I'll never have to see Marc Riley again.'

'Never have to see who again?' a bright voice queried.

Camira looked up and laughed. 'Come in, Jane. Don't tell me you walked over too? Everyone seems to be crazy about walking these days.'

Jane Sinclair let herself in through the screen door and sank down into an armchair. 'I've escaped,' she said dramatically. 'I might not even go back. Put me up for . . . the next ten years, Camira love?'

Camira studied the pert little face beneath its boyish thatch of orange hair and the now matronly figure of her best friend and said affectionately, 'You've got to be the happiest prisoner I've ever met.'

Jane passed a hand over her burgeoning stomach and said with a sigh, 'Sometimes. Well,' she brightened, 'almost always. Today was just one of those days. I think the twins are teething. Either that or they're sickening for some mysterious disease, like meningitis or scarlet fever.'

'Jane!' Camira protested. 'You can't be serious.'

'Not really, love,' Jane conceded with a rueful grin. 'But have you ever noticed well, obviously you haven't yet, but your turn will come,' she warned darkly and went on, 'All these baby books one reads seem to have these comforting little riders telling you never to take what appear to be teething symptoms lightly *just* in case! So then you read on and on, and before long you've convinced yourself it's got to be something fatal!'

'What does Alan reckon?' Camira asked with a grin. Alan was Jane's husband, a big man and seemingly more so in contrast to his wife's lack of inches, who said little— another striking contrast. He was a professional fisherman in a small way, with his own boat, and Camira often wondered what had attracted these two such diverse characters in the first place. But there was no doubt Jane was devoted to him. And although he was probably the least demonstrative man Camira had ever met, just occasionally she had surprised a look in his eyes as they rested on his bubbling, vivacious wife which had surprised her with its intensity.

Jane pouted. 'Alan,' she said deliberately, 'threw the book out of the window.' Then she caught Camira's eye and chuckled. 'He's putting them to bed,' she said, referring to her nine-month-old twin sons. 'He told me to come over here and have a good cry if I wanted to, and tell you all my problems and not to go back until I felt better.'

'Right.' Camira stood up and put the kettle on. 'Tell away. But before you start, what do you want, tea or coffee?' She turned. 'Or some fruit juice? Perhaps that would agree with number three child better?'

Jane giggled and patted her stomach again, which was now revealing her fourth month of pregnancy. 'You're as bad as he is,' she accused. 'What I really wouldn't mind is a good stiff drink. However, I shall not indulge.'

'You're right, you won't,' said Camira, 'because I don't have any, apart from the fact that I wouldn't allow you to. Have to be content with a cup of tea. Now, you can start crying on my shoulder if you want to.'

She carried the cup of tea to Jane and took her own to the table.

'I never had any intention of doing that,' Jane said indignantly. 'Besides, I'm dying of curiosity, Camira. We all are. Alan's actually met him, the lucky so-and-so, but you know how forthcoming Alan is.'

'I take it,' Camira said dryly, 'you're referring to Marcus Riley?'

'Of course I am! What's he like?' Jane said eagerly. 'The whole village is agog, you know.'

'He's all right,' Camira shrugged, and went on counting money stolidly.

'Camira,' Jane warned, 'don't make me cross now. That's not very good for my delicate condition either, you know.'

Camira looked across at her friend and knew there was no way of escaping her probing inquisition. Jane had a passionate love of life and an insatiable curiosity about everything and everyone that went hand in hand with it. Better to get it over with, she thought to herself and was annoyed to find that her palms had turned suddenly sticky as she recounted a pile of dollar notes.

She put her head on one side and said casually, 'He's wealthy, good-looking—I'd say he'd be about thirty. He appears to be unattached.' Although not alone, an inner voice prompted. The girl Lisa had still been there until Saturday at least, Camira knew, but she'd seen very little of her. As little, fortunately, as she'd seen of him.

'Go on,' Jane prompted.

'I guess you could say,' Camira shrugged, 'he's one of life's beautiful people. Although I must admit,' she added, and hoped fervently she could keep a grudging note out of her voice, 'he has a reputation for being a top trainer and what I've seen so far bears that out.'

'Did you know he was a show-jumper . . . when he was younger, I suppose,' Jane offered. 'But he gave it all up when he turned to training thoroughbreds. He used to play a lot of polo too, apparently. You must have heard of him?'

Camira froze. Of course! Marc Riley! *Why ever* didn't I connect the two? Perhaps I am vegetating, because anyone with any interest in show-jumping would know it. Know it, yes, but did you actually ever see a picture of him? Perhaps the Marcus put you off. Perhaps. . . .

She came back to the present with a start. Jane was staring at her assessingly.

'Don't tell me you didn't know, Camira?'

Camira laughed a little shame facedly. 'I didn't. And if I had, I'd have mentioned it to you for sure! What a co-incidence!'

'Yes, isn't it', Jane said thoughtfully. 'Have you told him how good you are?' She waved an impatient hand at Camira's sudden restless movement. 'Oh, I know your mother would never allow you to compete, but for all that you were really top-flight. Even . . .' Jane hesitated and then said boldly, 'even David knew that. And he was very good himself.'

Camira clenched her jaw for a moment. But she said quietly, 'It's something you can never *know*, unless you do compete. And anyway, I wouldn't be very good now.'

'Why not?' Jane demanded. 'Old Mr Thompson used to let you keep your hand in on that horse he retired to be a hack. It would only be about three . . . maybe four months at the most since you rode.'

Camira managed a slight smile. 'Three months too long, Jane. Besides, I . . . what I mean is, with someone as good as he was it could be very embarrassing.'

Jane chewed her lip. She said finally, 'If he's such a . . . how did you put it . . . beautiful person, why do I get the distinct impression you don't like him?'

Camira flinched inwardly. She never had been able to keep anything hidden from Jane. It would have been far better to have said straight off that she hated and detested the man. But then I would have had to tell her the details, she reminded herself, and couldn't suppress a slight tremor from passing through her. And that I couldn't do . . . not that.

So she said baldly, 'As a matter of fact, I don't really go much on him. I don't know why. Some people just affect you that way, don't they?'

'Alan seemed to take to him. Not that he said much about him. But I've learnt to read between the lines.' Jane grinned. 'Maybe, because you're working for him, he mentioned that to Alan, by the way. Maybe he's the kind of person who sort of likes to keep employees in their place?'

'Maybe,' Camira agreed, and breathed a little easier. And

eager to change the subject she reached over to the book case and picked up a pink box. 'I've never given you back your notepaper, Jane. Do you remember the day when I was desperate to write that letter and you came to the rescue?' She added to herself, I remember it very well even if you don't.

She'd run out of notepaper herself and a walk to the local store had proved fruitless, so she'd called in at Jane's on the way home to borrow some. Jane had been only too anxious to help and she had firmly over-ridden all Camira's doubts upon seeing the only notepaper she was able to produce, a boxed gift set that had been a Christmas present from her teenage sister tastefully adorned with delicate violets and roses.

Camira had tried to object, but Jane had said forcefully, 'Don't be silly. A letter's a letter, it's what you put in it that counts. And anyway our Land Rover's in for a service, so I might not be able to drive you into to Pimpama or Beenleigh for days! And don't you dare walk,' she had added fiercely. 'And don't look like that either! If I can't repay you for all the honorary baby-sitting you've done by doing a few errands for you when I go shopping—well, I don't deserve to have you for a friend.'

So Camira had walked on home clutching the pink box and only wishing it wasn't quite so flowery and delicate and rather nauseatingly scented and cursing herself for forgetting to put a plain-lined writing pad on her last shopping list. She'd still been doubtful after the letter was written and sealed, but when the mail man called the next morning she'd snatched it up impatiently and given it to him, mindful of Jane's words: It's what you put in it that counts. . . .

Jane stirred now in the armchair and reached for the box.

'Thanks, love.' She added mischievously, 'I must have been right, mustn't I? I mean, you've obviously been able to arrange the water and everything else quite satisfactorily, despite my pink notepaper!'

Oh, Jane, Camira thought, if only you knew how wrong you were! And with such good intentions too. But I'm not at all happy with the water arrangement. And thanks to your pink notepaper . . . well, she amended, not entirely, but it certainly didn't help. However, at this point her thoughts seemed to grow rather chaotic, so she made a deliberate effort to switch them off.

She jumped up and said brightly, 'I've just realized I'm starving. Like to share a snack with me? Or are you watching your figure?' she asked on a gentle note of fun, knowing Jane was always hungry.

'Love to!' Jane replied, and poked her tongue out playfully. 'I am eating for two, you know.'

'Or is it three?'

'Don't!' Jane objected laughingly. 'Two sets of twins would just about finish me!'

Monday morning dawned rather earlier than Camira would have liked it, but nonetheless she arrived at the stables as a faint lightening of the eastern sky forecast the dawn and a cool breeze brushed the dew-damp grass against her jeans. It often was cooler around dawn than the deep hours of the night, she knew from long experience, and at this time of the year in the subtropical climate of south-east Queensland it was almost always the only cool time of day or night. Which was one reason why the horses were worked so early.

A slight tremor of apprehension ran through her as she paused at the double stable doorway and cast a last lingering look around. Last week Marcus Riley hadn't been much in evidence down at the stables and his foreman Bob Duffy, a likeable ex-jockey with a tiny wizened face that reminded Camira of a monkey, had been in charge. However, this week could be different, something warned her. There'd been still so much to organise and arrange last week, but from today, I wouldn't be surprised if we get down to business in earnest, she thought. And twelve horses in full work . . . it's a lot of work. Her eyes lingered on the broad sweep of the training track with its white-painted railing that was now visible in the growing light and she thought inconsequently, it's a beaut track, considering it's a private one. As I should know. In fact I feel as if I know every inch of its twelve-furlong surface.

She closed her eyes and could feel with every fibre of her body that incredible sensation of speed and power when you had a good horse beneath you and you were crouched on its neck with the soft morning air flowing past you. . . .

She turned and shook her head to rid it of those imaginary hooves pounding on the turf and with a deep breath pulled open the door and marched in.

To find her worst fears immediately confirmed. The first person she laid eyes on was the one she least wanted to see. He was walking towards her down the long central passageway that ran between the horse stalls in the large stable shed, leading two horses.

She tensed immediately, but could not prevent a very faint pink colour from rising to her cheeks.

He appeared not to notice it, though, and said quite impersonally, 'Morning, Camira. Can you take these two and get them saddled straight away. They're scheduled for an easy work-out. And as soon as it's light, saddle up Mission Beach and Good Time Gal. They'll be getting a good hit out.'

She nodded as he handed her the two leads. He turned away.

And Camira was intensely relieved, as the morning wore on, to find that this brief exchange was to set the tenor for all further communications that passed between them.

She worked steadily saddling horses up and then unsaddling them as Bob and the young apprentice called Marty brought them back from their work-outs. And then there were stalls to be done, feeds to be mixed and the whole host of chores that attend the preparation of horses.

Fortunately she'd found that she and Bob had established an early rapport and even Marty, who was an unprepossessing and pimply youth on first sight, had turned out to be a cheerful, likeable kid who was easy to work with. This was the full complement of paid staff, herself, Bob and Marty, but Tim had been a regular helper last week as well as this morning, as was his brother . . . today. Of the lovely Lisa there was no sign.

Camira couldn't help admiring Marc Riley, albeit unwillingly, as the morning wore on. She was honest enough to realise that this state of mind was no doubt due to the fact that she now knew who he was—a much respected show-jumper and an ace polo-player. Of course he didn't ride any of the horses, that task was reserved for Bob and Marty, but his mastery of them was apparent in everything else he did. They led better for him, they suffered the indignity of having their feet minutely inspected with a minimum of fuss to his touch, and they suffered the indignity of drenching via a nostril tube also with a minimum of fuss when he did it. And Camira, who was no mean hand with horses herself, had to acknowledge this. She found it didn't bring her much comfort, though.

It was Mission Beach, a tall fine-drawn gelding, who

came back from his work-out looking visibly distressed. Camira found she was holding her breath as she led the horse around in the yard beneath both Bob's and her employer's acute gaze.

Marc said, 'Did he eat up last night, Camira?'

'He left about three handfuls.'

He turned to Bob. 'Did he feel as if he was tied up, not stretching out? Lame? Anything?'

'He seemed to be labouring over the last furlong, Marc. Matter of fact he didn't feel, you know, strong like he usually does. I tell you I was quite surprised, because he had an easy week last week. Should have been jumping out of his skin. What d'you reckon?'

Marc shrugged, but didn't take his narrowed eyes off the horse as Camira led him patiently around. 'I can't see that he's lame. There's no heat, no swelling in his legs and his last blood count was damned near perfect. You're sure he didn't get on the wrong leg taking the turns? He might have overreached or something.'

'Marc,' Bob said plaintively, 'I ain't some green novice. I'da known.'

Marc grinned briefly. 'Okay,' he said resignedly. 'That means we've got to proceed to the theory that he's picked up some flaming virus. And you know what that means, Bob, don't you?'

'Yeah,' Bob spat out the stalk of hay he had been chewing. 'It means getting a blood sample out of the bastard.'

The full import of those words didn't strike Camira until a short time later. Mission Beach, it appeared, had a pathological dislike of having so much as one drop of his blood withdrawn however good a cause it was in, and he resisted mightily from the very moment the hypodermic syringe came into to play.

Marc said forcefully, 'I swear he's telepathic. I haven't even got within a foot of his jugular and he starts playing up. All right now, everyone, let's make a concerted effort. Tim, you put the 'twitch on, Bob, you hold up his foreleg, Marty, you make sure he doesn't back out of the bay and pull the chain off the wall and you hold his head for me, Camira. Watch yourself,' he added briefly to her.

Camira did, but she was more concerned with holding the horse's head still, which was how, several straining, sweat-soaked minutes later when it was all over, she came to grief. Her employer had located the large jugular vein and managed to get the needle in and was in the act of withdrawing it when Mission Beach gave a heave that forced Bob to release his foreleg and Tim to loose his grip on the twitch. Mission Beach then shifted sideways and brought his offside, not small, forefoot down fairly and squarely on Camira's own foot.

She gulped and for a second her grip on his headstall slackened, but fortunately for her Mission Beach shifted again just as she felt her foot must be ground to nothing.

'There!' Marc held the full syringe with its bright red contents up to the light. 'Okay, you can relax, folks.'

'You all right, Camira?' Bob asked. 'Did he stand on you?'

Marc, who had turned away, swung back and noted the sudden pallor of Camira's cheeks. 'I told you to watch yourself!' he said in exasperation. 'You need nimble feet in this game.'

'It's nothing,' Camira said calmly. Not that she was feeling particularly calm, but she knew she'd die rather than admit it . . . to this man anyway. 'Shall I wash him down and put him away now?' she offered.

'If you're sure you're all right,' he said roughly. 'You don't need to indulge in any heroics, you know.'

'I'm sure,' she said flatly, and so saying she unclipped the chain from the headstall and backed the horse out of the bay and led him to the wash-bay, willing herself to walk without the slightest vestige of a limp.

She must have been convincing, she decided, because she could feel his scrutiny through the back of her shirt, but after a moment he turned away and she heard him say to Bob.

'Put this in the fridge, will you, and as soon as you've finished here you'd better get it to the vet and have him test the white cell count.'

But several hours later when she was back in her own home and gingerly removing her boot from her poor foot, Camira couldn't help wondering if she'd been very wise. Her instep was black and blue and feeling peculiarly mangled. There can't be any bones broken, she reassured herself, or else I wouldn't have been able to stay on it this long. But I sure am going to feel like limping around for a few days to come! What I need is a good bran poultice.

It was while she was so engaged that Tim came to call on her. He took one look at her foot now resting in a large bowl of water and the assortment of packets and so on lying beside her on the carpet and said immediately as he closed the screen door behind him,

'Why on earth didn't you tell us, Camira? I know just how painful it is to have a great big horse stand on your foot.'

Camira smiled at his note of boyish concern. She hesitated, unable to think of anything diplomatic to say. 'I . . . I . . .'

'I know,' Tim said with a sudden grin, and plonked himself down on the carpet beside her to inspect her foot minutely. 'Marc gets me that way sometimes to. He kinda

makes you feel . . . small, if you know what I mean. But I
sometimes wonder . . . when he gets prickly like that, if it
isn't because he's concerned really?'

'Maybe,' Camira agreed, and decided there and then she
liked Tim more than any teenage boy she had ever met, although she didn't tell him that in her opinion, the last thing
Marcus Riley would have felt was concern, for *her*.

'What are you going to do to it now, Camira?' he asked
as he put her foot back gently in the water.

'I'm going to use an old recipe of my grandfather's on it,
Tim—a warm bran mash, Epsom salts and a few other odds
and ends. I know it works for horses, so it should work for
me.'

'You're good with horses, Camira, aren't you?' Tim said
seriously. 'I can see it and I heard Bob telling Marc it the
other day. He said you were the best sheila he'd ever had
working for him, Bob did. Marc'll realise it to,' he added
earnestly. 'As soon as he . . . as he. . . .' His voice trailed
off and a sudden look of anxiety and confusion flooded his
young, freckled face.

Camira said gently, 'As soon as what, Tim?'

'Oh, nothing.' He stood up and then said brightly, 'Can I
make you a cup of tea or something? I like your little house,
you know,' he added as he looked around and then bit his
lip as if mentally castigating himself for having jumped
from one awkward subject right into another. 'I'm sorry,
it must be awful for you after . . . after owning Camira.'

'It was once, but it's not any more, Tim,' she said warmly
and not entirely truthfully but determined to put him at his
ease. 'As a matter of fact, since you mentioned tea, I've just
realised I haven't had lunch and I'm starving! Would you
like to join me? It's only bread and cheese, but the bread is
homemade and I've got some homemade pickles and straw-

berry jam and some cherry cake left. Will they expect you back home for lunch?'

'Oh boy!' Tim grinned, and licked his lips. 'Sounds great. I doubt if they'll miss me at home. She's leaving tonight, by the way, did you know? Lisa, I mean.'

Camira said nothing, but she couldn't help realising that she subconsciously echoed Tim's tone of relief. I wonder why, she asked herself honestly as between them they assembled lunch and sat down at the table. I really wonder why. But she didn't pursue it, because what Tim was saying suddenly took her full attention.

'My jumpers are arriving tomorrow, Camira, did you know? Together with Marc's polo ponies. And he's promised me that I can erect some jumps in the middle of the track to practise on. Have you ever had anything to do with show-jumpers, Camira? I've got a new one. . . .'

Bob was her next visitor and he arrived at about four o'clock in the afternoon with a definite mission.

'You should have told me, Camira,' he said reproachfully, as she hobbled to the door to greet him.

She sighed resignedly. 'I suppose Tim told you? Does . . . Mr Riley know?' she asked as she ushered him in.

'He must, I reckon,' Bob drawled, and added with infinite logic, 'seeing as how it was he who told me. Personally like. Also told me you're to have the day off tomorra.'

'But I can manage!' Camira objected spiritedly. 'Look, it's not the first time a horse has stood on my foot and it probably won't be the last. I'm coming,' she said mutinously.

Bob surveyed her thoughtfully for a moment and then said, 'Camira, how old are you, love?'

She compressed her lips. 'Twenty-*one*!'

'Hmmm,' he commented. 'Should have thought by that age you might have recognised a Force Ten gale when you saw one. Listen, love, what he says goes! It ain't no use trying to buck him because you're liable to end up with far worse than a sore foot if you do. And he says no dice! You're to stay put here tomorra and nurse yourself back to full fighting fitness. Do yourself a favour and take heed of an old-timer, will ya, kid? Just do as he says.'

Camira subsided somewhat. 'Was he . . . very angry, Bob!' she asked tentatively.

'Nah! He was . . .' he shrugged, 'very contained, if you ask me.' He grinned suddenly, an impish, mischievous grin, his eyes alight with laughter. 'The fact that he banged every door he could lay his hands on might easily have been because her ladyship is leaving us tonight, so I'm told. Easily!'

Camira swallowed and shivered as if someone had walked down her spine. 'I suppose I was a bit silly,' she admitted.

'You was,' Bob agreed. 'Although for sheer guts I've gotta give you ten outa ten. But listen, Camira, okay, so he may have his ways—we all do, I guess, but he's all right. You do the right thing by him and he'll come up trumps every time. Take my word for it, I know,' he said with particular emphasis. 'And something else, just in case he ever forgets to mention it to you himself, you got sheer magic in your hands, kid, when it comes to horses. I'd lay you London to a brick on you're something else when ya get to ride 'em. I know,' he said again, 'I seen 'em, the good and the bad, the ones who think they have it and the ones who don't ever have to think about it. You're one of those. A born horsewoman if I ever saw one.'

'A born horsewoman?' Camira asked herself the next mornas she pottered painfully among her vegetables. She couldn't prevent a small thrill that the repetition of Bob's words brought. 'But nevertheless,' she scolded herself, 'a lame one.'

The following day brought her back to work, still slightly lame which she was unable to hide much as she would have loved to. Her employer was again very much in evidence, but after looking her up and down coldly when they first met and once referring to her as 'Hopalong Cassidy' he made no mention of the incident.

Camira was relieved but slightly chilled as it became increasingly obvious that Marcus Riley was in a foul mood and that they were all bearing the brunt of it. On my account, she told herself as she stoically raked out the stalls and resolutely shut her ears to the hard words Marty was on the receiving end of, over something really trivial. I ought to apologise to them, she thought, but when she tried to do just this to Bob some time later, when things had quietened down somewhat, he looked at her in surprise.

'Now what gave you that idea?' he asked.

'Well . . . you said he was wild with me,' she stammered.

'Sure he was—then. But that ain't his way, kid. If he blows up he does a thorough job of it and then it goes one of two ways. You're either out on your ear or he makes your life miserable for an hour or two and that's the end of it. He don't carry grudges for days on end. Not for the people who work for him.'

Camira digested this. 'Well, why is he so mad, then? I thought it might have been seeing me again that triggered it off.'

Bob removed his cap and mopped his brow with his forearm. 'You reckon he's mad today? You shoulda seen him yesterday!' He grinned at her. 'Nah,' he said, 'it ain't you.

If you ask me it's his love life that's getting to him. I'm told,' he went on with a conspiratorial wink, 'that her ladyship kinda got the mistaken idea he was putty in her little clawed fists. She couldn't have been more wrong, kid, I can tell you. I seen many of 'em get the same idea, but they learn, sooner or later. Matter of fact she lasted a bit longer 'an most, which could account for it. This mood, I mean. He mighta thought he'd found a fair dinkum sheila this time.' Bob chuckled and shook his head. 'I coulda told him, but still, I'll be the first to admit it's often hard to look past the . . . well, I guess you get my drift, Camira?'

Camira nodded and had to grin herself.

Bob went on, 'So don't you worry your head about it, love. He'll be back to normal in no time. Never takes him long. By the way,' he added casually, 'had a good look at Tim's jumpers yet?'

'Not yet,' said Camira. 'I might on my way out. I'm due to knock off—unless there's anything else you want done?'

'Uh-huh,' he said, and shook his head. 'You run off home—rather limp off home,' he amended. 'See you to-morra, love'.

Camira did as she was bid and on the way down the long passageway she paused and hesitated for a moment in front of the adjacent stalls that housed Tim's jumpers. She'd had no contact with them as yet because Tim did it all himself. But instead of inspecting them eagerly as she was dying to do she turned on her heel abruptly and walked on.

If she'd had eyes in the back of her head, she would have known that Bob was still watching her with a very thoughtful look on his unusually serious face.

CHAPTER FOUR

IT was a week later, during which, as Bob had predicted, Marcus Riley returned to normal, that he said to her as she finished work one morning,

'Come up to the house with me, Camira, will you? There's something I want to talk to you about.'

She hesitated and her nails dug into her palms for several reasons, but finally she nodded. 'I'll just put these saddles away,' she murmured, as much to give herself time to think as because the job needed doing. It was normally Marty's chore.

'I'll see you in about ten minutes, then?'

She nodded again. What could it be about? she wondered a little wildly. During the last week they'd all worked in perfect harmony, and if he'd been slightly . . . distant with her, she'd been only too grateful for it. Well, she admitted wryly to herself, almost grateful. And yet just on the odd occasion she'd felt a twinge of . . . was it regret? Perhaps, she allowed honestly. There was no doubt Marc had a vital, likeable personality and she had little difficulty in understanding just why Tim and Bob and for that matter Marty were unusually devoted relations and employees.

It's just that I feel on the outer, she thought as she donned her inevitable straw hat and walked towards the house. But she hardened her heart almost immediately as she recalled the night he had visited her. You really have to be a man to appreciate Marcus Riley, she told herself. If you're a girl with any sense at all you'd run a mile.

Now, Camira, she warned ruefully, just because he's irresistible to most females, it doesn't mean you have to assume you're cast in the same mould. Far from it. All it means is that he's a very experienced man and he could probably wring a response from a stone statue!

Which was so much in line with what she had told herself repeatedly after that disastrous night she had to smile to herself.

So what is it he wants to see me about? she wondered again. I'm quite sure he's forgotten I even exist from that point of view. It can only be because he's not satisfied with my work and he wants to terminate the contract. She closed her eyes briefly as she trod up the front steps. Dear God! What will I do now?

It was Mrs Leonard who opened the front door to her. An energetic, motherly widow, she obviously thought it her life's mission to take care of the Rileys' practical, day-to-day needs. Just how she had regarded the lovely Lisa and her counterparts, Camira couldn't imagine. Or rather, yes, I can, she corrected herself. He's cast his spell on her too, just like Bob and Marty . . . but he needn't think. . . .

What he needn't think, she never told herself because by that time Mrs Leonard had ushered her into the study and left, admonishing them that she'd be back in a tick with a cup of tea.

Marc Riley was writing at the desk and he said with a quick upward glance, 'Take a seat, Camira, I won't be long. He added, as he dropped his eyes to the desk, 'I'm glad to see you're no longer limping.'

Camira sat with gritted teeth. Presently he finished writing, by which time her overwrought nerves had manifested themselves in several ways. She had clenched her hands in her lap and then she had retrieved her hat from where she had laid it on the floor, and if it couldn't be said to be already in a rather mangled state, it certainly was now.

Marc dropped his pen and lounged back, his eyes narrowed as he scanned her face and the evidence of her discomfort.

He said finally with a faint grin, 'What's up? Did you imagine I was going to leap on you and attempt to ravish you?'

'If I did, it wouldn't be without cause,' Camira said grimly.

He laughed openly at that, his wide shoulders shaking slightly beneath the blue-checked cottonwork shirt he wore with faded but well-fitting twill trousers, and if it was possible she hated him all the more because he looked so much the part.

I suppose he always does—a despairing thought that caught her unawares. Whatever role he's playing, he'd fit into it superbly.

He said leisurely, 'No, not today, I think,' quite as if he were rejecting a dessert. 'Actually, I wanted to talk to you about the party.'

Camira was caught unawares. 'Party? What party?'

'The one I'm giving this weekend. A housewarming, I suppose you could say. I have several friends both in Brisbane and on the Gold Coast who tell me they're dying of curiosity to see my new acquisition. Also, everyone I've met round here has been particularly friendly—well,' he amended with a slight narrowing of his eyes, 'almost everyone, and very helpful too. I'd like to reciprocate. This weekend seems the best choice because from next week on the horses will be racing, and I'm sure you know what that means.'

Camira said confusedly, 'Yes, but I don't see—I mean, why do you need my help?' Particularly as we've now established I'm the only unfriendly person in the neighbourhood, she added beneath her breath.

'You know everyone around here and although I seem to have met most of them, I really can't remember all their names. I thought you wouldn't mind helping me to compile a guest list.'

'Everyone!' Camira exclaimed in surprise. The village was a very small hamlet, but if you took in the neighbouring cane farmers that accounted for about fifty souls providing you didn't include their offspring. She blinked.

'Why not?' Marc said lightly. 'I thought we could barbecue a couple of sheep or something. Bob's a dab hand at it. And put on a keg or two of beer. Do you think they'd enjoy it?'

'They'd love it,' Camira said honestly. 'What about your friends, though? Might they not think it a bit rustic?'

'Why should they? They're people too, and just about everyone I've ever known loves a good country shindig . . . once in a while at least. And that's the beaut part of being situated here. It's only an hour's drive from Brisbane and about the same from Surfer's Paradise.'

'I meant,' she said crossly, 'we're really rather simple folk down here. Fishermen, cane farmers,' she shrugged, 'the odd retired couple and several men who work for the Main Roads department. Might not *we* seem too rustic for your friends?'

'And myself, you were no doubt going to add. Tell me, Camira,' he said on a steely note that should have warned her, 'when you were the belle of the district, as I'm reliably informed you were several years ago, did you distinguish between people solely on account of their occupations? Did

Miss Johnston of Camira Lodge sort out the sheep from the goats?'

'I . . . of course not,' Camira said heatedly.

'Well, why are you so ready to assume that I'm like that, and my friends?' he shot at her.

'I don't . . . I didn't,' she stammered.

'Yes, you did,' he said shortly, and stood up. 'What the hell,' he muttered with an abrupt gesture. 'I can do without your help and your peculiar notions about . . . just about everything,' he added with a mocking glance.

Camira swallowed. 'I'm sorry,' she said as she studied her hands. 'I don't really have peculiar notions. I didn't mean it to sound quite like that.'

'Didn't you?' he said with sardonically raised eyebrows. 'I could have sworn you did. How *did* you mean it to sound?'

She bit her lip, conscious that she had allowed her dislike of him to lead her into an untenable position. She *had* meant it to sound exactly as it had. She hadn't bargained for the fact that he would dissect it and make it stand to be seen for exactly what it was. But I should have known, she thought wearily. I should have known. . . .

She said quietly, 'All right, I apologise unreservedly. It was a nasty thing to say.'

She met his hazel gaze squarely and for a moment thought he wasn't going to accept the apology. Here it comes, Bob, she told herself. I'm about to be turfed out on my ear! And she held her breath.

But Marc moved at last and shrugged indifferently.

At the same time a light tap on the door sounded and Mrs Leonard walked in bearing a tray.

'Here's your tea, loves. And some of my chocolate cake. Not as how I'm too confident of it, though,' she said to

Camira. 'Because from what Tim's told me, I guess I'll have to look to me laurels. He was right wrapped up in your cherry cake, not to mention your homemade bread. What do you think about the party?' she continued on the same breath. 'A great idea, isn't it but?'

Camira was forced to murmur agreement.

'Well, I'll leave you two young things to get on with the planning of it,' said Mrs Leonard with all the heavy-handed wisdom of her perhaps forty summers, and added brightly, 'By the way, Camira, tell 'em all to dress up a bit, will you? I really feel like wearing me best dress and giving the old feet a bit of a twirl. You are going to have some kinda music, aren't you, Marc? You wouldn't be so stuffy as to hold the kind of party where all the men sit on one side drinking beer and all the sheilas sit on the other side talking kids, now would you?'

'I never have, Mrs Leonard,' he answered with mock gravity. 'I don't see why I should start now.'

'No, well, mind you don't, love. Because I tell you I've had me eyes on Bob Duffy for a few years now and this might just be the opportunity to nail him!' And she did a few dance steps with an exaggerated flourish before she passed through the doorway with the time-honoured Queensland salute. 'See you later!'

Camira couldn't help herself. She burst out laughing. 'Does Bob . . . do you think he knows?'

'I wouldn't be at all surprised. In fact I'd lay you London to a brick on,' they smiled at each other at the use of Bob's favourite phrase, 'he not only knows but he's playing coy.'

Camira said, still grinning, 'I wouldn't have thought it of Mrs Leonard. I mean, she's a real character, isn't she?'

Marc sobered. 'Is she, Camira? She's honest, she's reliable, she'd lay down her life for me or Tim. Especially Tim because she's known him since he was a baby. But you label her a "character". Something a bit odd? To me she's warm and real and she's earned every penny I've ever paid her and much more besides, that I'll never be able to pay her because there's no *way* you can pay for the services she's rendered. Things like loyalty, for instance. So she's set her cap at Bob? He's not the first and perhaps he won't be the last. Does that just wipe out all the rest? Does that automatically make her worthy of no more than a chuckle?'

For once Camira found that her own eloquence didn't desert her. She said steadily. 'Believe me, I don't take the Mrs Leonards of this world lightly. If anything I marvel at them and envy them more than you'll ever know.'

'It's very simple, then,' he said seriously, 'if that's the case. Just let go. Have trust. The worst that can ever happen to you is that you have a good laugh at yourself after you've shed a few tears. You start again.'

She stared at him. 'Is that the way it happens for you?' she said bitterly, incredulously. 'I once knew someone like you. I doubt if he ever so much as shed one tear. He laughed . . . all the way to the bank, probably. But he caused more heartache than you would have believed possible. And it wasn't the kind of heartache you could shrug away with a few tears. In fact it's partly because of him that I'm now sitting in this chair. . . .'

She broke off and looked around painfully. As had the Thompsons, so had Marc Riley taken over the beautiful, mellow old furniture that was so much a part of Camira House. Some solid, some dainty and a lot of it crafted from cedar. It had been a lifetime hobby of her grandmother's collecting, restoring and caring lovingly for it.

'. . . This chair,' she went on flatly. 'Do you know I used to climb into this chair from the time I could walk?' She shrugged. 'And for that matter all the chairs in this house. But now I sit in it and worry myself silly in case I'm about to be fired. Perhaps I should shed a few tears and laugh. Maybe one day I might. But when I see you and I see the way you treat women and then I hear you talk about having trust and being this and being that. . . . Oh, you're so right, if you did but know it. It's really . . . only laughable.'

She stood up, her cup of tea still on the desk in front of her untasted. 'I'll make up a list and bring it round tomorrow morning. No, don't bother to see me out,' she added gently, although he hadn't stirred. 'And don't try any of your Boy Scout tricks on me either. It just might backfire today.' She swung on her heel.

'Camira!'

But she didn't even accord him a backward glance.

She spent the rest of the day weeding and hoeing and pruning and watering, and was mildly surprised to find that she had no trouble banishing the morning's confrontation from her mind. It was almost as if a veil had dropped on it and successfully blotted it from further retrospection.

'A good thing too,' she told herself as she inspected her watch and decided enough was enough. 'All these dramatics are getting a bit tiresome . . . as much for . . . everyone else, probably,' she added ruefully. She stuck her spade into the ground and rested her foot on it. 'What happened to your cherished serenity, Camira Johnston?' she asked herself with a light grimace. 'I mean, it is all rather long ago, isn't it? You've lived with it for three years now, most stoically. Why this sudden breaking out?'

But she found she shied away from answering her own question.

She spent nearly an hour soaking in the tub and when she

got out she gave way to an unusual impulse and instead of her normal brief toilet, she got out a bottle of carefully hoarded and wildly extravagant body lotion and smoothed it into her skin from her shoulders to her toes. Then she applied a moisturiser to her face and neck and spent nearly fifteen minutes brushing her thick, smooth, shoulder-length hair that was the colour and texture of light beige silk, and instead of twisting it back into the knot she usually wore, she let it hang free tucked behind her ears as she attended to her nails, thinking at the same time that since she didn't do this very often, she might as well go the whole hog.

It was as she'd just finished this chore and was admiring the smooth rosy ovals, unpainted but perfectly shaped, and reminding herself never to get lazy and give up the gardening gloves she wore, not only for gardening but for the more mucky horses chores, that a car drove up and stopped beneath her window.

So sure was she that it must be Jane, the only person she knew who made a habit of visiting her after dark, that she turned the small transistor beside her down, and called out lightly, 'Come in, you two. Or is it three? I'm in my bedroom making myself beautiful. I don't quite know why,' she added with a deprecating grin. 'How was your day?' She turned towards the sound of footsteps. 'Mine was. . . .'

She stopped in mid-sentence, her lips still formed about the words, and with a hasty movement she pulled her dark blue robe beneath which she wore not a thing more closely around her and stumbled up.

For it wasn't Jane who had strolled into her bedroom but Marc Riley.

'Hellish?' he supplied with a streak of sheer devilry in his dark eyes as he took in her suddenly pink cheeks. 'Your day, I mean,' he said with that blend of mockery and amusement that she was coming to know so well. 'Who are these two or three people you're expecting?' he asked curiously. 'Do I know them?'

'Yes. No. I don't know,' she said disjointedly, aware of all things of how he seemed to make the already small room look smaller.

He grinned at her. 'That sounds like a similar imposture to the one you adopted over whether you were a good cook or not.'

'I mean——' she said tartly. 'What I mean is,' she began again, 'I was expecting my friend Jane—*she's* expecting a baby, you see, but the last one she was expecting turned out to be twins. So we tease her sometimes.'

'Do you now?' he said with honest amusement. 'And what time are you expecting her?'

'I'm not,' said Camira, and then could have bitten her tongue. 'I . . . she does very often pop over in the evenings, though. I thought it must be her.'

'Good,' he said unexpectedly. 'I'm glad you don't have a fixed date with her. And I'm glad you're making yourself beautiful, because I've come to take you out to dinner.' His eyes roamed over her as she stood suddenly transfixed. He said with a quirk to his lips, 'That's a very fetching robe you have on, but it might not be quite suitable for a restaurant.' He waited for her to say something, but she found she was quite incapable of speech and with a low laugh he threw the jacket he'd been carrying over his shoulder on to the bed and stepped towards her wardrobe.

'Just a minute,' she burst out. 'What do you think you're doing?'

'I was going to find you something to wear,' he explained. 'As you see, I'm only casually dressed. That's one good thing about Surfer's, they don't go in for a lot of formality.'

'I . . . I. . . .' she spluttered as she involuntarily took in what he was wearing—a dark brown silk shirt atop cream linen trousers, and the jacket he'd flung on the bed was of a beautiful rich supple suede, severely tailored and also cream. She tore her gaze from his handmade leather shoes and thought incongruously that he might think himself casually dressed but she had no doubt he could go anywhere in those clothes. This thought crossed her mind just seconds before she said, also involuntarily,

'You're crazy! I'm not going anywhere with you. And don't you *dare* start rummaging in my wardrobe!'

He took his hand off the handle and stepped towards her. She backed, but almost immediately felt the edge of the bed behind her. And he kept on coming.

When he was right in front of her she found that her stupid, treacherous heart had started to race as she was suddenly aware of how her body was betraying her beneath the fine cotton of her robe.

If Marc noticed, and she was positive he must have because his dark glance raked her up and down and lingered then on the swell of her breasts for a fleeting second, his reaction came as a surprise.

He said evenly, 'Camira, we've had one little spat today. Let's not make it two. All I have in mind is sharing a good meal with you and perhaps getting you to air all the grievances you've bottled up so tightly for the last years. At least, that's all I have on my mind at the moment. But if you continue to fight me every inch of the way, who knows, my . . . *Boy Scout* tendencies might come to the fore, because I'm determined to take you out to dinner tonight and I could easily be moved to dress you with my own hands. It's a simple choice you have really.'

'You wouldn't!' she gasped incredulously.

He laughed coldly. 'Oh, wouldn't I? Shall we put it to the test? Or have you forgotten what happened the last time you said that to me?' He leant past her and picked up his jacket from the bed. 'Seeing that you're almost there, so to speak, having already been engaged in making yourself beautiful, I'll give you—twenty minutes? I'll wait in the lounge.'

And he closed the door behind him with just one completely impersonal glance.

Camina stared helplessly at the closed door. Several rash, wild plans came to mind. Like for example locking herself into the bedroom until he tired and went away. But this was no good, because if there ever had been a key to the bedroom door, it wasn't there now. She transferred her eyes to the window, but that was no good either. It was an old-fashioned sash window, easy enough to scramble out of and not that high off the ground, but the wire screening set there to frustrate the hordes of mosquitoes and sandflies was firmly clipped into place, from the outside, so as not interfere with the opening and closing of the window. Short of cutting it with some sharp instrument. . . .

'No!' She gave herself an impatient shake. 'I'm certainly not going to destroy a perfectly good screen,' she told herself, sotto voce.

Which really left her with no alternative, she realised. She took a deep breath and counted to ten, then slowly walked to her wardrobe and opened it wide.

Considering the other sparsities of her life, her wardrobe was surprisingly well filled. Oh yes, she reminded herself, and wrinkled her nose faintly. Plently to choose from, but all of it at least three years out of date and smelling faintly of lavender and camphor. But surely there must be something that was at least the right length. Her hand hovered uncertainly and then came to rest on a classically cut and timeless silk blouse in a pale plain grey that seemed to echo her eyes. It was quite severe in its cut apart from the short sleeves which were slightly puffed and then gathered into a narrow band. She searched on and finally withdrew the skirt she normally wore with it. This was of a fine crêpe, fully lined and cut on the A-line, and the greys matched almost identically.

Now if I can find the belt, she thought, I'll be right. But the belt she had usually worn with it remained elusive. She could visualise it perfectly. It was suede, about two inches wide and a brilliant aquamarine colour, and it had two long tassles that hung down the front of the skirt and was the perfect foil for the all-over grey.

Oh well, she shrugged philosophically, who cares anyway? But another thought brought her up short. Shoes! She might not look desperately out of date with this outfit, but her shoes would give her away immediately. Or would they? she wondered, as she withdrew a pair and surveyed them doubtfully.

These shoes were dainty high-heeled sandals with a delicate sling back and as a matter of fact they were Jane's cast-offs. Recent cast-offs and almost brand new, but Jane had been quite determined that they made her feet, which were the same size as Camira's, look chubby, and all Camira's protestations had failed to convince her otherwise.

'You have such slender feet, Camira,' she had said enviously. 'I know mine are the same length, but they *look* fat in those shoes. You have them.'

'I'll never wear them! I mean, the colour for a start—you'd have to have a special outfit to go with these shoes.'

'Nonsense,' Jane had replied briskly. 'What's wrong with the colour? It's beautiful, and any neutral colour would go

with them. Now don't argue!' Which was a frequent phrase
Jane applied to Camira.

It *is* a neutral colour, Camira thought as she looked down
at herself now clad in the pale grey outfit. Perhaps amethyst
shoes don't look so bad with it after all. She stared down at
her feet with her hands resting on her hips. And another
thought stirred at the back of her mind. Her grandmother's
rings.

She pulled open a duchess dawer and withdrew a small
wooden carved box. She selected two rings and slid them
on to the little finger of each hand. Both were silver, one a
round filigree band and the other a narrow band of silver
that widened slightly on the top of the finger and supported
three tiny amethysts. She stretched her hands out and
couldn't help admiring the touch of elegance the rings
brought to them.

But a knock on the door interrupted these reflections and
she heard him say through the panels, 'Time's up, Camira.'

'I'm coming! Just a second.' She stood in front of the
mirror and inspected herself anxiously. She'd applied a
minimum of make-up—mascara and lip gloss and the merest
hint of a pale violet eyeshadow. And her hair was neatly
coiled behind her head again. She lifted her arms suddenly
and adjusted the back of her collar so that it stood up. It
makes me look a bit sophisticated, she thought. Then she
grabbed a hanky and tucked it into her sleeve. She turned
back and gave herself another spray with the expensive
perfume Jane had given her for Christmas—Jane was like
that; she gave wildly impractical gifts that you couldn't
help but adore even if you had no use for them.

The click of the door opening jerked her upright and she
turned tensely to meet Marc's no doubt critical gaze.

And he did inspect her critically from the top of her head

to the tips of her toes with his hand still resting on the door handle until she couldn't prevent a faint colour rising from the base of her throat and she said tartly, 'I'm sorry if I don't come up to your usual standard.'

'But you do,' he drawled. 'At least,' he amended as he crossed the room towards her, 'you've . . . almost exceeded my expectations.'

A slight frown creased her brow as she wondered what he meant.

He smiled lazily at her and went on in the same undertone, 'I'd like to make just two adjustments.'

And before she realised what he was about, she felt his hands about her neck as he turned the back of her collar down and smoothed it into place. For a moment his hands lingered and she was supremely conscious of them through the thin silk.

'That might suit . . . Lisa,' he said. 'It doesn't suit you.' He laughed gently as her eyes blazed at him, and said imperturbably, 'Neither does this.' With a swift sure movement he probed the knot at the back of her head with his long fingers and deftly removed the pins so that her hair tumbled about her shoulders.

Camira gasped as he ran his fingers through it and would have retreated, but he took her by the shoulders and turned her towards the mirror.

'I think you wear it like that as a defence,' he said quietly. 'But it makes you look older, you know. Besides, it's criminal to hide such beautiful hair.'

She stared at their two reflections in the mirror. He was still standing behind her with her shoulders beneath his hands and with that tinge of amusement and mockery just beneath the surface, as he looked down at her. It was her own reflection that caused her to draw a swift breath.

I look a little dishevelled now, she thought. As if I've been kissed, or. . . .

Her lips parted suddenly. As if I've just got up out of someone's bed. *His* bed. And with a swiftness and clarity that took her completely by surprise she found that the reflection in the mirror had dissolved and been replaced in her mind's eye by one of the two of them, in bed, with her fair hair mingled with his and her arms caressing his strong, smooth tanned shoulders. I know very well what they look like, she thought shakily from the first morning I met him. . . .

She shut her eyes swiftly to dislodge this powerful, mind-bending image and when they flew open again it was to see in the mirror that he was still looking down at her, but intently now, with narrowed eyes and his mouth set in a grim line.

Then he looked up and their eyes clashed in the mirror.

He stepped back and dropped his hands casually into his trouser pockets. 'Shall we go?' he said evenly.

'Yes,' she answered abruptly, suddenly in a panic almost to escape her own torturous thoughts.

It wasn't until they were half-way to Surfer's Paradise that her hands flew to her head and she remembered that she hadn't re-combed her hair.

She smoothed it anxiously with her hands until Marc flicked her an impersonal glance and said briefly, 'I told you, 'it looks fine.'

Camira folded her hands in her lap, willing them to stay still as he sent the car hurtling along the dark Pacific Highway.

I just wish I could do the same with my thoughts, she told herself a trifle bitterly. Because if I think what's happening to me is really happening, I'm going to need all my defences about me. I can't . . . I just can't believe it's anything more than a game to him. A game that he *can't* resist playing with any woman who isn't a one-eyed freak, perhaps. And with Lisa gone and really nothing but horses to fill his life now, is it any wonder he's casting around for someone to take her place?

But you've achieved *something*, Camira, she added to herself. All right, it's humiliating to have to admit it, but you've finally admitted that you can—you can be physically attracted to a man you detest. Now, what you've got to do is just hold the thought that it's no more than a transitory mechanism your body controls quite separately from your heart and mind, and if you can, use that knowledge as a tool to fight him with.

She grinned suddenly, a tiny wry grin. Forget the word fight, Camira! Vanquish is a better word. Because from now on you won't offering any provocation at all. Simply a blank unspoken resistance. . . .

She looked around as the car slowed and nosed into a parking place in the heart of Surfer's Paradise and realised that her thoughts had carried her through most of the journey.

CHAPTER FIVE

PERHAPS it was with those same thoughts in mind that she said flatly a little later, 'All right, I'll tell you.'

She moved her empty plate to one side and glanced around. The restaurant Marc had brought her to was dim, discreet and very expensive. It also had a very long-standing reputation for fine food and the empty lobster shell on her plate bore mute testimony to this. It had been delicious, as had the avocado au vinaigrette she'd had to precede it.

A waiter materialised at her side to remove her plate and another to refill her wine-glass.

She rested her fingers on the stem of the glass and watched the golden liquid swirl gently. A pianist was, seemingly idly, coaxing soft sensuous music from a gleaming black grand piano, and all around great vases of flowers gave glimpses of their beauty in the candlelight. And on each table was set a small vase containing just two blooms of the exotic, waxy flower that was almost an integral part of the Gold Coast, in all its many colours and from which this restaurant took its name.

She moved and cast her companion a swift glance. But he was still sitting patiently, relaxed and turned towards her in his chair with one arm thrown over the back of it.

'It all started with my mother,' she said expressionlessly. 'She wasn't an evil, wicked person. She was beautiful, engaging, and for the most part of my life I adored her. But she and my father were . . . mismatched, I suppose you could say. He was . . . he wasn't dominating or domineering. And he was perfectly happy with his life at Camira and quite prepared to take the good with the bad. He also adored my mother. But she was a different kind of person. She loved having people around her, parties, expensive clothes. And she loved being able to do the unexpected. I can remember once when she chartered a plane and took some friends to see Ayers Rock by moonlight. . . .

'And for a long time, they seemed to be able to bury the differences in their personalities. While there was plenty of money and the prestige that Camira brought her, she could do all the things she wanted to and at the same time be a . . . I think he thought so anyway . . . a good wife to him. But all the same, we *all* knew there was an . . . implacable streak to her. It didn't surface very often, but when it did, it was almost impossible to fight.'

Marc said, 'So you coasted along as do most families in this imperfect life—until the money well dried up?' he queried perceptively.

'How well you put it,' she commented. 'To be honest, she wasn't the cause of the original rot that set in. For a long time it was as if we were jinxed.' She shrugged. 'But it did look as if we were going to pull out of it and we would have, I'm sure, if my mother hadn't panicked. She was so used, you see, to being able to afford most of her whims. And . . . I don't know if I can explain it, but she had such a powerful personality we accepted all her extravagances as if they were just a natural, lovable part of her.'

'Go on,' he murmured as the pause grew.

Camira squared her shoulders. 'By then,' she went on, 'the combination of her and the several bad years we'd had meant . . . there wasn't very much in reserve. It was obvious we would have to tighten our belts to pull through. And that's what panicked her. She just . . . couldn't do it.'

She stared across the room unseeingly for a moment and then continued huskily, 'That's when she turned on the full power of her personality and somehow or other she coaxed and cajoled Dad and Grandpapa to take out a large mortgage on the Lodge and turn the place into a stud.' She lifted her shoulders. 'It did look as if it might be a success at first. We got plenty of mares on our name alone, but then, as they sometimes do, yearling prices plummeted and our first crop of progeny turned out to be a fairly hopeless lot. It seemed our stallion was an expensive flop, things became desperate and there was no choice but to sell Camira.'

She sipped her wine as the silence lengthened.

Marc poured himself some more wine and said finally, 'That still doesn't explain what you said to me this morning. You haven't told me about this man of whom I remind you so much. The one who laughed all the way to the bank.'

She took a deep breath and reminded herself of her earlier resolution. She said calmly, 'He and I were engaged. Unfortunately, my mother had managed to keep our . . . difficulties a very closely guarded secret. But the day came when even she couldn't prevent it from leaking out. When he found out he came to me and told me in a roundabout kind of a way . . . anyway, what amounted to this—while he'd been quite prepared to marry Miss Camira Johnston of Camira Lodge and incidentally the sole heir to it, he wasn't quite so happy about marrying Miss Nobody Johnston of Nowhere. He proposed a different kind of liaison, one that would be just as enjoyable, he said, but we'd both benefit from not being tied down by it. He was a little older than I was.'

She couldn't prevent the bleak look that came to her eyes as she raised them to Marc's gaze.

'Go on,' he said again. 'I presume you told him what he could do with his proposal?'

'Yes,' she said steadily. 'He wasn't a great deal put out, as it happened. Or maybe he was, I still don't know. Perhaps he *was* threatening me. He didn't drop us immediately, but he started to pay a lot of attention to my mother. She was only in her late thirties and still very, very attractive. I don't know, under normal circumstances I don't think she'd have given him a second glance,' she said painfully.

'But under those circumstances she did? And more?' he offered.

Camira nodded and swallowed stiffly. 'And she was so used to my father seeming not to notice her ... sillier notions, I honestly think she thought he hadn't realised what was going on. But I knew he had. And even though it hadn't moved beyond the flirting stage,' she winced, 'I was desperately afraid it would.'

'And I wonder what you did about it, Camira?' he asked softly.

'I didn't have to do anything,' she said evenly. 'Fate intervened, as it happened. My father planned a little treat for my mother on her birthday. He'd kept up his licence and he borrowed a friend's plane and planned to fly her up to the Darling Downs—she was born up there—and spend the day paddock-hopping between the properties of people she knew, those with air-strips anyway. But,' her voice faltered for a moment, 'but the tension he'd lived with for several years plus the awful thought of losing my mother were too much for him. He had a massive heart attack at the controls of the plane and they crashed into the range. They were both killed instantly.'

Marc said slowly, 'Not a pretty story. But I don't altogether see what there is about me that brings this man so forcibly to mind. What became of him, by the way?'

Camira flinched. 'He came to see me after the funeral. I think he was appalled at the way things had turned out. He tried to tell me so, anyway. He tried to tell me he'd never been serious about my mother, it had only been my refusal to go and live with him that had made him a little ... unbalanced. I think that was the word he used. He even had the gall to ask me to marry him and tell me he wanted to look after me for the rest of my life. . . .'

She clenched the stem of her wine-glass with whitened knuckles as she realised her words had caused Marc's shoulders to shake suddenly with suppressed laughter.

She said fiercely, 'If you think it's *funny*. . . .'

He grinned fleetingly. 'I was only wondering what you went to hit him with.'

Her face burned.

He said curiously, 'Had you ever slept with him, Camira?'

She gritted her teeth. 'What do you think? I suppose you imagine. . . .'

Marc interrupted smoothly. 'No, I don't think you did,' he said consideringly. 'Which was probably why he acted as he did. He was—possibly—desperate to get you to bed.'

'He could have,' she pointed out coldly. 'When he broke off the engagement we were due to be married in a couple of months' time. Was it too much to ask him to wait that long?'

'Sometimes, yes,' he said slowly. 'And sometimes when men have lust in their hearts they don't behave quite rationally. Unfortunately girls don't always realise this when they set out to attract.'

Camira frowned and then burst out. 'If you think I . . . teased him and led him on! Is that what you're insinuating?'

'No, I'm not. I'm sure you were very prim and virginal and very careful not to do anything that would unleash a flood of primitive passion. And that, my dear innocent Camira, is a most potent attraction in itself—although some of your sex have lost sight of it.'

She wetted her lips. 'Do you mean,' she said suddenly curious herself, 'that's how . . . you like it?'

He laughed at her. 'Sometimes.' He shrugged. 'It has an added spice to have an intensely private relationship with a woman who doesn't flaunt herself blatantly even just by the clothes she wears. But when you close the bedroom door, all that reserve she shows to the rest of the world disappears.

For your eyes only.'

She shivered involuntarily.

She said, 'I thought men liked to be able to flaunt their women. You know, the kind of attitude that says 'Look at my wife—or mistress—if I can attract such a beautiful, obviously sexy woman, I must be all right!'

But as the last words left her mouth she regretted having said them because of the grim, angry look that he suddenly directed at her.

And then it was gone, to be replaced by the old satire. He shrugged. 'It comes back to what you consider sexy, I suppose. But I'm sure you wouldn't generalise about all women. Why should you do so then about men?'

'Because on the evidence, it's hard not to,' she said tartly. But a warning sounded in her brain. I'm getting out of my depth, she thought, and into just the kind of confrontation I should be avoiding at all costs.

So she said quietly, sincerely, 'Thank you for a lovely meal. Shouldn't we think of getting home now? Dawn comes very early at this time of the year.'

Marc's teeth flashed and he said laughingly, 'You're so right, Camira.' And she knew instinctively that he'd seen through her little ploy to disengage herself from the conversation. He looked at his watch. 'It's not really so late, though. What about trying out that new disco that's just opened with such a blaze of publicity?'

'Disco,' she said blankly.

'Yes. Have you never been to one? In small doses and provided they're not too assaulting on the eardrums, it can be fun. Especially after a meal when you're feeling a mite lethargic and if you can really let yourself go to the music.' He added, 'I can recommend it. And when you've had your fling, you come away feeling relaxed with your skin slightly damp and all your inhibitions packed away for the moment. And then a good way to end an evening like this is to go for a stroll on the beach in the moonlight and let the cool breezes play on you.'

Camira amazed herself at the way she handled this. I couldn't have done it better than if I'd written it out and learnt it by heart! she thought.

'It sounds great,' she said lightly. She put her head on one side. 'Perhaps I'll take you up on it—one night when I don't have to rise with the kookaburras and pick tomatoes by torchlight.' She stood up, smiling. 'Really, I'd like to go home now.'

Marc stayed where he was, looking up at her, his hazel eyes bright and perhaps a little appreciative. 'So you've switched to Plan B, have you, Camira? Well, maybe you're right. For tonight anyway.' He stood up and ushered her courteously ahead of him. And all the way home he was deferential, charming company, but he said nothing that even a man could have construed as personal and he dropped her at her front door, waited until she'd unlocked it and switched on the lights and then driven off with a murmured goodnight.

Camira stood in the middle of her living-room and bit her lip as the sound of the car faded.

He's not only detestable and super-confident, he's also far too clever for his own good—or rather for my peace of mind, she thought. I shall have to be very, very careful.

It *was* Jane who visited her the next evening, bubbling over with enthusiasm too.

'Camira,' she said exuberantly as she sank down into an armchair. 'Tell me all about this party, love?'

Camira grinned at her over the ironing board which was

set up in the lounge on account of the lack of space in the kitchen.

'So you got your invitation?'

'*Personally* delivered, would you believe! I nearly fell flat on my face. Isn't he just gorgeous!'

'I suppose he is,' Camira murmured, still smiling faintly. 'Are you and Alan going to come?'

'Going to come?' Jane echoed. 'Of course we're going to come! And the twins will be no problem, because he said we can put them to bed upstairs and check on them any time we like.'

Camira's smile faded somewhat at this, because Jane's twins had represented a very slight chance of evading this forthcoming party. Camira always babysat them. But it seemed now that she had absolutely no excuse. Not that Jane would have agreed anyway, she told herself with a tiny lift of her shoulders. She turned the blouse she was ironing and started on the front.

'So tell me exactly what it's going to be like, Camira.' Jane settled herself more comfortably and looked across the ironing board with an air of expectancy.

'Well,' Camira said assessingly, 'Bob—he's the stable foreman, by the way—apparently lived in Tonga for a while. I suspect there aren't many places Bob hasn't either lived in or visited. Anyway, he claims he's a dab hand at preparing a fair dinkum Tongan feast as he calls it. So instead of the traditional 'barbie' so beloved of us Aussies, we're going to have roast suckling pig cooked over coals in pits dug in the ground. And as an accompaniment we're to have paw-paw and mangoes and avocado pears and of course prawns and lobsters. I gather Alan's been roped in to provide them fresh.'

She stopped, because Jane's eyes had been growing

rounder and rounder. But she closed them before they popped and said dreamily, 'It sounds just *mouthwatering*! This
will be one night, Camira, when I shan't mind the thought
that I might be eating for three. Now tell me, what does
one wear to a Tongan feast?'

Camira hesitated, suddenly mindful of Mrs Leonard's
words. 'Well,' she temporised, 'I think you could wear a
long dress, provided it wasn't a ball-gown, you know, or, a
jump-suit or that snazzy pair of harem pants you bought
last year to go with that thing you called a boob-tube,' she
said teasingly.

Jane cast her eyes heavenwards. 'Them days have gone,
love, and they might never return if what I look like now is
anything to go on. But,' she added seriously, 'I do have a
long dress, it's only cotton—what the glossies refer to as a
patio dress—but it does make me look less . . . well, just
less,' she said with a grin. 'Do you think that would do?'

'On you, it would be perfect,' Camira said with quiet
sincerity.

Jane said warmly, 'Thanks, mate.' She added, 'What
about the blokes? I reckon there'll be a fair amount of speculation even among them over what to wear. Some might
even be moved to turn up in a collar and tie!'

Camira grinned to herself and interpreted this remark
correctly to be a feeler put out by the village folk through
their appointed spokeswoman. She said quite seriously,
however, 'I don't think that would be necessary. But on the
other hand, there are people coming down from Brisbane
and up from Surfer's, so I don't think shorts and a singlet
and thongs would be quite right. Say, trousers and a sports
shirt? Do you think they'd mind?'

'Oh, not at all,' Jane said hastily. She added honestly and
with an impish smile, 'They'll only be too happy to know

what's the order of the day.'

Camira hung her blouse on a hanger and reached for another. Here it comes! she warned herself. Unless I'm much mistaken. . . .

She was not.

'You know,' Jane said thoughtfully, 'you said you didn't go much on him. I really can't help wondering why?'

'Neither can I,' Camira said casually. 'It just goes to show you can't always depend on first impressions. He's . . . really good to work for. I think,' she said seriously, 'I was just a little bit worked up about someone else coming on to Camira. I'd got so used to the Thompsons, you see. By the way,' she rested the iron, 'there's going to be music, a tape deck or something set up under the house. D'you think you could pass the word round that it would be appreciated if people danced?'

'Oh, not at all!' Jane said vibrantly. 'It'll be a pleasure, in fact. Hey, I was always enthused about this party, but it gets to sound better and better! Camira. . . ?'

'What?' said Camira.

'Oh, nothing,' Jane replied with an unusual lack of eloquence. She heaved herself up out of the chair. 'I suppose I ought to hie me off home. Back to prison,' she said brightly. 'And by the way,' she turned at the front door, 'don't you dare go walking to this party and climbing fences, because we'll pick you up and deliver you in some kind of style. If it's the last thing we do. See you later!'

And Camira was left with the uncomfortable notion that her best friend Jane was perfectly alive to too many unspoken inferences. Although how . . . just how? she wondered.

CHAPTER SIX

THE rest of the week passed in a flurry of activity at Camira Lodge and Camira found herself irresistibly drawn into it. Mrs Leonard consulted her on the preparation of the food, particularly the local delicacies, and when she discovered that Camira's strawberries were ripe she immediately commanded her employer to buy the whole crop. Which under any other circumstances would have delighted Camira, but when she discovered she was to be paid far too well for them, she dug her heels in and for a moment it appeared as if a battle royal would ensue.

It was Mrs Leonard who saved the day. She took a quick look at Camira's hot face as she gazed at the amount of money in her hand and another quick look at her employer's implacable expression and said brightly,

'I've just had a great idea! Tim tells me you make the most fabulous pavlovas, Camira. How would it be if you supplied some *with* the strawberries? Nobody can resist strawberry pavlova, and it would just solve the problem of what to have for dessert nicely!'

And that had settled that, although Camira was aware that Marc Riley continued to look at her with some irritation for the rest of the day.

It was Tim's job to set up the concreted area under the house as the dance floor, and Camira found her opinion sought on how to decorate it, what kind of music would be best and so on.

'Well,' she said to Tim, 'I suspect we're a little bit backward around here when it comes to the latest dances, so why don't you start off with all the old-fashioned ones that every one knows and loves, like The Pride of Erin—that would certainly get the locals on to their feet. And then when we've loosened them up you could slip in the more modern disco stuff? Sound like a good idea?'

'Sounds great,' Tim grinned at her. 'You're a fountain of wisdom, Camira. I suppose you've helped organise something like this often?' And he blushed immediately at the implication of his words.

'Once or twice,' Camira agreed gently. She went on to ease his embarrassment. 'How's your new horse coming on, by the way? I've been so busy this week I haven't had time to watch.'

She couldn't have hit on a better subject, because Tim straight away forgot his discomfort and told her about all the problems he was having with his new horse.

She asked, 'What does Marc say? You surely couldn't have a better adviser.'

Tim sighed heavily. 'Matter of fact, I did something a bit silly a few weeks ago, Camira,' he admitted. 'Remember when Marc was in a bit of a mood after Lisa left? Well, I got into a mood too, you see. And when he was giving me some advice—you know how he can be sarcastic and cutting about it, sort of?'

'When he's in a mood? Yes, I know.' She smiled. 'Don't tell me you told him what to do with his advice?'

'I did,' Tim said guiltily. 'Rather strongly.'

Camira laughed and thought, good on you, Tim! But she said, 'I'm sure you only have to apologise. He could be feeling as guilty as you do for being in such a mood in the first place.'

'I know. It's just not as easy as it sounds to make the first move—Camira, have you ever jumped horses?'

But Camira retreated hastily. 'Not seriously, Tim. Is that Mrs Leonard calling? I think it is. I'll come back and help you with this.'

She left, unaware of the curious look he gave her.

Finally it was the night of nights. Camira didn't bother much with her own appearance, but then at the last minute before Jane and Alan were due to arrive, she stood in front of the mirror and studied herself critically.

Having passed the word on about what was suitable apparel, she had taken her own advice and was wearing what she presumed would also qualify as what Jane termed a patio dress. It wasn't new, but it had been thoroughly aired and pressed and like the grey outfit she'd worn, the design had an almost timeless quality to it. It was cut very simply, a button-through front all the way to the hem from the neckline, which sported a small upstanding Chinese collar, and it was sleeveless. But the austerity of its plain fitted lines was relieved by the material itself—a silky cotton with surprising body in it, in a shade of pale, clear turquoise which looked cool and fresh and seemed to invest her eyes with a slight tinge of its colour.

Once again she had the amethyst sandals on and her grandmother's silver rings.

'Jane was right,' she murmured to herself as she studied her reflection, 'they do go with a lot more than one would have imagined.' She narrowed her eyes and put her head to one side. It was a nice dress and it made her look slender in all the right places. 'But it's not a . . .' she sought for the right word, 'not a flaunting dress exactly. Perhaps . . . even prim? I wonder. . . .'

An engine and a horn sounded outside and it was too late to do any more than wonder. She gave her hair, which was loose save for two smooth wings looped round to the back of her head and secured with a matching turquoise slide, a final pat and called, 'Coming!'

Jane said reproachfully as Camina climbed into the car beside the two kiddies' seats attached to the back seat and each containing an identical, chubby, shining, and at this moment, gleefully chortling occupant, 'I don't know how you manage to look so cool, Camira. I feel hot and bothered and I know I look a mess!'

Camira's eyes met Alan's for an instant in the rear-view mirror and he closed one in a slight wink. She said soothingly, 'Wait until we've got these two poppets to sleep, pet, then you can have a quick tidy-up and you'll feel like a million dollars. I'll give you a hand and we'll get them down in no time at all.'

Jane looked grateful and slightly shamefaced. 'Sorry, folks,' she said, 'but it's like trying to organise an army, fair dinkum!'

Camira was as good as her word and with Mrs Leonard's help she and Jane were soon installed in a spare bedroom and Masters Gary and Peter Sinclair were both engaged in the solemn task of having their last bottle of the day, each ensconced on a carefully fenced-in bed. Fortunately this last bottle seemed to have a very soporific effect and Peter even fell asleep before he'd quite finished.

Jane sighed with relief. 'It always works,' she said wonderingly in the now dim room. 'Thank heavens! Do you think they'll be all right, Camira?'

'I'm sure they will. They're used to sleeping through a bit of noise, aren't they? And anyway, we'll check up on them every now and then. Do you feel ready to face the fray?'

Jane giggled as she pulled a comb through her hair. 'Ready as I'll ever be. Okay, let's go.' And they slipped out quietly. 'Here we are,' Jane said as she handed Camira a small plastic bottle. 'I know it doesn't quite go with Joy, but you'll be eaten alive if you don't rub some on.'

Camira accepted it and dabbed some of the insect repellant on herself.

Jane said, 'You know, some enterprising person should come and live among the mangroves and maybe they'd be able to come up with a more seductively perfumed repellant. I'm sure it would go well!'

They were both laughing at this as they came out on to the verandah. The sun had set now, but the area below was brightly lit at the bottom of the front steps and quite crowded.

Camira's smile faded as she stood poised at the top step with one hand on the railing and one hand to her skirt. It's too much, something inside of her said. This is just too much to see Camira like this again. But another inner voice took over. No it is not, it said calmly. You can cope with this.

She turned her head to Jane and said steadily, 'Ready?'

But Jane was staring past her, down to the scene below the steps as if riveted. Then she lifted her head to Camira and wetted her lips uncertainly.

'What is it?' Camira asked anxiously. 'Don't you feel well?'

'I feel fine,' said Jane with a little tremor in her voice. 'But do you see who's down there?'

Camira scanned the crowd below quickly and shrugged. 'A lot of people, most of whom we both know. Come. . . .'

But Jane interrupted, 'Yes, a lot of people we both know. Including David Thorpe. Camira. . . .'

Camira gasped and her grip on the rail tightened painfully. 'He can't be,' she said faintly.

'He is. He's seen you too. As a matter of fact he looks about as stunned as you do.' Jane said a trifle grimly. 'Although why, I can't imagine.'

'Where is he?' Camira asked breathlessly. 'I can't . . . oh yes, I can.' Her grey eyes rested on an upturned fair head. There was something about the owner of the head that was making him conspicuous to his companions now, something in his stance that reflected acute surprise and tension as he stared up at the verandah, and she saw Tim and Marc Riley who were beside him glance at one another curiously.

She said tightly to Jane, 'What can I *do*?'

'Do?' Jane said gently, and put her arm through Camira's. 'We'll go down these stairs as if we haven't a care in the world, that's what you can do. Because if you run away from him now, Camira, he'll read more into it than there is to be read. Don't worry, Alan and I will be with you every step of the way. Now smile, love. Show him you don't give a damn!'

Which I don't, Camira reminded herself dazedly as she and Jane walked down the steps and were immediately engulfed in a throng of laughing, cheerful people and as if summoned by an invisible signal Alan loomed up from nowhere with two long, cool drinks in his hands.

But the pattern of the party swirled and eddied colourfully around Camira as the locals were introduced to the newcomers, and she knew it wouldn't be long before she would have to face David Thorpe. At least let it be on his own, she found herself praying, because if Marc hadn't already gleaned the connection, he would quickly enough. . . .

Her prayers weren't answered, though, because it was Marcus Riley who shepherded David through the crowd towards her. She saw them coming, stopping frequently to talk to people on the way, which gave her plenty of time to marshal her defences—or would have if she hadn't found suddenly that they'd deserted her completely and all she wanted to do was turn and run. But Jane and Alan stood solidly beside her like guardian angels and all she could do was study the two men as they advanced slowly but so inexorably towards her.

No one could deny that David Thorpe was good-looking. He wasn't quite as tall as his companion, but he had the same kind of air. Smooth elegance that didn't quite hide a hint of controlled power just beneath the surface. In David's case, his fairness was deceptive because his skin was tanned deeply and any association with a pink and peeling sunburnt image that so often went with fair hair was dispelled.

Why, oh, why didn't this possibility occur to me, Camira wondered shakily, before I bared my heart to Marc like an idiot? They've probably known each other for years. Because if Marcus Riley had been a top show-jumper and polo player, David still was.

She clenched her hand round her glass as they drew nearer, conscious that she was feeling almost sick. It was Jane who saved the day.

She said softly with a quick upward glance at Camira that was full of amusement and mischief, 'Here he comes. Don't brain him with your glass or anything, will you, Camira?'

And that did it. Camira found herself relaxing almost involuntarily and found too that she could barely repress the giggle that rose to her lips. Really, she thought, I must curb this fighting image everyone seems to have of me. Here they are!

'Camira,' said Marc Riley, 'and Jane and Alan. It's good to see you. I'd like you to meet a friend of mine.'

But before he could make the introductions David interjected, 'As a matter of fact, old son,' he said, 'I know Camira and Alan and Jane. I *thought* it was you two standing at the top of the steps! How are you, Jane?' His blue gaze rested thoughtfully on her for a moment and then he transferred it to Camira and shook his head and laughed boyishly. 'I must say you could have knocked me down with a feather to see you of all people here, Cam!'

She flinched. She'd forgotten David's private name for her. She'd found it rather endearing once, probably because her mother had always forbidden anyone to shorten her name. Now it only grated.

His tanned face grew serious. 'You do know how miserable we all were for you, Camira? That's why it came as such a surprise, I guess, to see you here. Are you . . .?' He let the question hang in the air.

'I bought back a corner of the property, David,' she found herself saying. 'In fact I never left Camira.' She shrugged. 'I don't think many people knew.'

'They didn't,' he commented on an oddly taut note. 'Is your grandfather still alive?'

Camira shook her head and swallowed a sudden lump in her throat.

Marc Riley said easily, 'Well, this is interesting. How did you two get to know each other in the first place?'

David turned to him. 'I'm surprised you don't know,' he said with a grin, 'seeing as she's your next-door neighbour, I presume. Camira was one of the most promising show-jumpers I ever saw. If her mother had allowed her to compete she would have been world class in no time at all, I can tell you!'

It was only a sudden stillness that betrayed Marc Riley's reaction to this statement. Camira saw it because her eyes flew to his face before she could stop herself. Their gazes locked fleetingly and then he said lightly,

'You've been holding out on me, Camira. And Tim. You only had to say, you know, and I'm positive Tim would have been only *too* delighted to have you up on one of his horses.'

Her voice sounded strange to her own ears. 'I'm really out of practice now. I don't think I'd be game—especially with you and Tim around.'

'But if you were that good,' he murmured, 'you'd pick it up again in no time. We must arrange something soon.'

Camira's eyes flashed for a moment and she was very tempted to say that nothing would induce her to ride for him, but she bit her lip and Jane coughed beside her while Alan stirred restlessly for a moment, but the most welcome diversion was created by the most unwelcome source.

A car had driven up unnoticed, but its occupants didn't remain so for long. They threaded their way through the crowd, a tall thin gangling man with a woman beside him. They were approaching from behind David and Marc, so it was Camira who saw them first, and her eyes widened incredulously, causing her employer to half turn and look over his shoulder. As he did, the woman ran the last few steps towards him and flung her arms around him.

'Marc!' she purred delightedly as she peeped provocatively up at him from beneath her long dark lashes. 'Just fancy that—Josh here rings me up and invites me to some do in the country, as he put it, so I agreed, and would you believe, it turned out to be your do! Isn't that a delightful coincidence, darling?'

Lisa's rather high-pitched voice seemed to draw a lot of attention, not the least from Bob and Tim who were standing not far away and who both now wore comically similar expressions of sheer annoyance. But it wasn't only their eyes that were drawn to this vision of loveliness standing so close to their host with her hands still on his arms, her dark beauty enhanced by a rather clinging, revealing dress that was strapless and a lovely shade of primrose yellow. It was as if the rhythm of the party had faltered, lost its beat and an unnatural quiet reigned for a moment.

In that moment Camira knew somehow that Marc Riley wasn't going to make a scene. For either of two reasons. Firstly because he was too sophisticated for it and secondly because as he stared down at Lisa for an instant, no one could mistake the sheer admiration in his glance.

So it came as no surprise to hear him say amusedly with a slight drawl, as he lowered his head to place a light kiss on her forehead, 'A delightful coincidence, Lisa.' He disengaged himself gently and turned to the tall man. 'Good to see you, Josh.' He held out his hand. 'You must meet everyone. Although I think you'll find you know a few. . . .'

And the rhythm of the party picked up its beat again as the cheerful, happy throng downed their drinks once more and looked admiringly towards the long, snowy-clad trestle table where Mrs Leonard and Marty were now laying out the food. And if anyone noticed that Mrs Leonard appeared to be banging the dishes around a bit it was only a very few of them.

Camira turned as if to drift away, but it was too late. It appeared that Lisa and David and Josh knew each other, but Marc had turned Lisa to meet Alan and Jane.

'And I think you know Camira,' he remarked.

Camira turned back unwillingly and looked straight into the other girl's dark eyes. Lisa was flushed and there was a curious look of suppressed excitement about her. But immediately her eyes narrowed faintly.

She said, 'Of course I remember you. Who wouldn't!' And she chuckled and put her hand conspiratorially on Marc's arm again and winked at him reminiscently. 'But I must say you look a bit different tonight!' she went on. 'Really, you look quite sweet tonight. I'm amazed. Marc,' she looked up at him obliquely, 'do you honestly think it's fair— I mean, I know she enjoys it, but do you honestly think it's fair to employ *Camira Johnston*, of all people, as a lowly stable-hand? I know you meant to be kind, but all the same, it's such a come-down for her, isn't it?'

Camira was conscious of several things. Of Jane spluttering and choking on a mouthful of her drink, of Alan's sheer open-mouthed look of bewilderment, of David's sudden restless movement followed by a look of disbelief. The one thing she didn't see was how Marc Riley reacted, because she simply didn't look at him.

She merely shrugged and said quietly, 'If you'll excuse me, I'll go and help Mrs Leonard.'

She helped Mrs Leonard throughout the entire delicious meal, despite that good lady's spirited protests. She relentlessly fetched and carried and served and cleared up, although Bob and Tim and Jane and finally even Marty beseeched her to desist.

'I'm all right,' she said with a laugh to each of them. 'Besides, it's so much the less for Mrs Leonard to have to do. And when it's done we can both relax and enjoy ourselves.' This to Bob. 'I'm sure you'll appreciate me then, mate,' she added with a tiny smile. 'I know Mrs Leonard will, once the music starts.'

'Now what do you mean by that?' Bob asked forcibly. 'I tell you, your running around like this isn't going to make the boss too happy.'

'Well, that's just *too* bad, Bob,' she said evenly, and left him staring at her, a picture of puzzlement.

It was David who finally brought her to a halt. He loomed out of the night on the back verandah just as she came out of the kitchen door, having made the last trip even she could justify as the last dishes were now cleared and the throb of music drifted up through the verandah floorboards.

'Camira!' he said roughly as she tried to pull away from him. 'You're not going anywhere until I've had a chance to talk to you. And this is as good a place as anywhere.'

Camira stared out into the darkness. On this side of the large house, if it wasn't for the music you could almost imagine there was no party, and she knew as if she could see in the dark that the broad sweep of the track lay just beyond the verandah. And beyond it, on a clear day you could see the cliffs of Stradbroke Island over the sea of low dark mangroves. How often, she asked herself, have I sat out here on the railing and watched those cliffs turn pink in the sunset?

She said, 'There's nothing to talk about, David.'

'Like hell there isn't! I'd just like to know what's going on. Do you work for Riley? As a strapper? Or is there something else you do for him as well? Something you wouldn't do for me?' he asked coldly, pointedly.

She said evenly, 'You have a one-track mind, David. You always did. I've never slept with him, but if I had it would be none of your business. *Least* of all your business.'

'Then why has Lisa Mackenzie got her claws well and truly into you?' he demanded. He added angrily, 'Believe me, I know her. She's got her sights set firmly on Riley—has since she first laid eyes on him. That can be the only reason. . . .'

'Stop it, David!' Camira said sharply. 'Is that the only thing that worries you?' she added bitterly. 'Obviously it is.'

He drew a ragged breath. 'It's not,' he said flatly. 'I want to know everything about you, how you've coped—everything.'

'You surprise me.'

'Do I, Camira?' he said slowly. 'If it's any consolation, I've surprised myself. You see, I thought I'd got you well and truly out of my system. Until I saw you standing at the top of those damned stairs. Then I knew . . . Camira. . . .'

'No, David,' she said firmly as he tried to take her into his arms. 'No.'

'Just—no?' he queried with a slight quirk to his lips. 'You were much more forceful the last time you said it, if you recall.'

She shrugged. 'It means just the same.'

'Has there been—anyone, Cam?' he asked softly.

'Yes. At least six,' she said baldly, then tensed as she heard his low laugh. ·

'I don't believe you. For a girl who's had six lovers you're remarkably unchanged.'

'That's nonsense,' Camira said heatedly. 'I must have changed some in three years. Anyway,' she added hastily, 'those kind of changes you don't see written in letters a foot high.'

'Some might not be able to see them,' he agreed quietly. 'But some sixth sense I have about you, my dear, makes me very sure you've not even had one—lover.'

'I hate you, David Thorpe,' she said dispassionately. 'And if you think after what you did you can force your way back into my life, you're quite wrong.'

'I wonder, Cam, I do. I think maybe where I was wrong was believing you three years ago. It's a long time for anyone to go without a mate. Especially a beautiful girl like you. There must be a reason.'

Camira stared at him for a moment unable to believe her ears. Then she turned swiftly and walked back into the kitchen and closed and locked the screen door behind her. It was a reflex action that led her footsteps through the kitchen and down a side passageway to stop suddenly outside her old bedroom door. Whatever am I thinking? she asked herself with a slight shake of her head. I must be mad! And she turned resolutely towards the front of the house, eager only to get out of it and all its memories.

But in the front hall she came face to face with Marc Riley. Oh, God! she thought. Not him.

It was none other, however. He didn't say anything, but he took her wrist in his hand with just one searching look at her face and drew her into the study. She started to protest, but he took no notice and only released her wrist when she was seated. Then he crossed to a cocktail cabinet and poured two brandies.

'You look as if you could do with it,' he said as he handed her one.

She took it, but refused to look at him.

He said, 'I apologise for Lisa. She was unforgivable.'

Camira took a gulp of brandy in sheer surprise and coughed as the fiery liquid slid down.

Marc grinned. 'You're supposed to sip it,' he advised. 'Savour it. It's very old.'

Camira cleared her throat and took a sip from the balloon glass.

'Good,' he murmured. 'Your friends are looking for you, by the way. I promised them I wouldn't allow you to do another stroke of work for the rest of the night. All your friends.'

Her eyes flew to his face. 'What do you mean?'

'I mean Bob and Tim, Mrs Leonard, David Thorpe.

There are a lot of people down there most concerned for you, Camira.'

She sifted through his words, but he'd mentioned David quite naturally and she breathed a small sigh of relief. If nothing else, the way David had handled their first meeting had been, she supposed, quite ambiguous, and so long as she could avoid him, or no, she thought suddenly . . . *force* herself to act quite naturally with him, and surely that wouldn't be too difficult in the crush of people down there. As long as she could get through the next couple of hours like that, she might just be able to maintain the charade.

She smiled at him. 'Thanks.'

'But we don't have to rush off. Finish your brandy. It's not a large one.'

She said, 'I think it's a great success—your party. All the locals seem to be having the time of their lives anyway.'

'Yes. And the best part is still to come. Tim's softening them up now, by the sound of it. He and Mrs Leonard have made a pact, I think, to get everyone on the dance floor. Young and old alike.'

'That puts Bob on the line.' Camira grinned.

Marc grinned back at her and said quizzically, 'Also you, my dear Camira. As a matter of fact I've picked out your first partner and I intend to keep a very close eye on you. Just in case you should cherish any notions of slipping home over the fence.'

Oh, what a lovely idea, she thought, and closed her eyes briefly in a moment of swift longing, but his voice brought her back with a start.

'I thought as much,' he said dryly. 'But it's not on, kid. You know, you amaze me, Camira. You never have any qualms about taking on more than you can handle, but when you meet someone on equal ground, you give up without a fight.'

'What do you mean?' she whispered.

'I mean, honey, Lisa's about your fighting weight.'

'I still don't know what you mean,' she said blankly. 'And don't call me that!'

'Don't you?'

'No! But if you think I should square up to Lisa Mackenzie because she treated me like she probably treats all females *you* come in contact with—well, you're crazier than I thought!' she said hotly. She eyed him angrily. 'And just what are you laughing at now, may I ask?'

'You,' he said. 'But anyway, that's better. I prefer to see you angry than with that sort of frozen look you had.' He stood up. 'Shall we go down now, Cinderella?'

Camira ground her teeth in frustration.

'Don't say it,' he advised gently. 'You might regret it.'

O.K.! Two can play at this game, she reminded herself, and you've slipped off the tracks once tonight, Camira.

She stood up and accepted his arm. 'Lead on, kind sir,' she smiled. 'Who's this partner you've chosen for me?'

'Why, none other than yours truly.'

Camira faltered, but she said nothing and she knew he was laughing at her again.

The rest of that fateful night passed in a whirl. Indeed, after her first dance with her employer, Camira did feel rather like she imagined Cinderella must have—bemused, unable to forget the feel of those strong arms around her, besotted in fact, she thought with a sharply indrawn breath as he surrendered her finally to Tim and said carelessly, 'Take good care of her, little brother.'

'I will,' Tim said seriously, and Camira felt as if she was

floating down off some cloud. Tim danced her very decorously around for a few minutes and then as the music changed he said eagerly, 'This is it, Camira. This is the hot stuff. Shall we show 'em how to do it?'

'I don't think I know how to do it,' she protested laughingly.

'Sure you do! It's so simple. Just follow me.'

It was a breathless half hour later before she finally called a halt. 'I'm exhausted and parched, Tim. I think I need a break.'

'Right. But you're going to dance with me again, Camira. Boy, oh, boy! For someone who didn't know how to do it, you sure catch on fast. Even Lisa's throwing you kinda death ray glances.'

Camira giggled.

Tim went on as he handed her a cool drink, 'Wow! Look at that old bloke,' he said admiringly as one of the Main Roads Department men went by. 'He sure learnt fast too! Mrs Leonard will be happy, I tell you.'

'I hope Bob is!' said Camira over the throb of the music, and they grinned at each other.

It was then that Camira suddenly remembered a little plan she'd had that she had somehow lost sight of in the course of the evening. She put her drink down. 'By the way, Tim, there's someone I want you to meet. Come with me.'

They threaded their way through the throng until Camira spotted who she was looking for—a pretty girl of about fourteen standing rather awkwardly between two adults.

'Julie,' she said, 'have you met Tim Riley? Tim, this Julie Gregory and her parents. They own the shop in the village.'

Julie Gregory flushed and clenched her fingers together as she murmured hello.

Camira went on, 'I know Julie's a fabulous dancer, Tim, because she won an award at the High School modern dance group, didn't you?'

Julie coloured again and looked as if she wished the floor would open up beneath her, but Tim said, 'That's great. Would you like to dance with me? I've never won any award, but Camira can vouch for me. I didn't stand on your toe once, did I, Camira?' He put out his hand and after a slight hesitation and still looking confused and selfconscious, Julie put her hand in his and he drew her on to the floor. He said something to her and after a fleeting upward glance, she smiled at him and seemed to relax somewhat.

Camira and the Gregorys also relaxed and then exchanged relieved glances.

'That was sweet of you, Camira,' Mrs Gregory said. 'Julie's so shy. He seems a nice boy, doesn't he?'

'He is, Mrs Gregory,' Camira said warmly. And I suspect, she added to herself, that he's going to grow and be just as devastating as his big brother in his own quiet way. Speaking of whom . . . she glanced sideways to find Marc Riley's eyes upon her from about ten feet away. He looked away and across the floor to Tim and Julie and then looked back at her and raised his eyebrows ironically. I wonder what that's supposed to mean, she thought. Disapproval? Surely not. But the rest of her reflections were halted as an arm circled her waist and a playful voice said behind her, 'Gotcha!'

'Oh . . . *Bob*,' she said laughingly.

'Only me,' he grinned at her. 'Who was you expecting?'

'No one!'

'Well, let's dance, then, shall we?' And he swung her energetically on to the floor.

From that moment Camira had no respite. She was danced off her feet and then some. As soon as one partner left her side another one appeared. Apart from Bob and Tim they were all village people, but it wasn't until she noticed Jane and Alan smiling very complacently at each other for no discernible reason that she realised the village had closed ranks about her, no doubt at Jane's instigation. David Thorpe was known to them all, as was everything that had ever happened at Camira Lodge, but David was given not the slightest chance of getting within a foot of Camira that night, and she felt unbearably touched at the loyalty of these people she had known all her life.

It was two o'clock when the party started to break up, and it wasn't a minute too soon for Camira, who was ready to drop. She and the Sinclairs said their farewells and gathered up the twins as the general exodus began.

Marc said to her as he shook her hand very formally, after kissing Jane and every other female goodbye, 'By the way, Camira, we're having a lazy day tomorrow. Come over about eleven, will you?'

Camira climbed into bed not long after and thought, well, that's been one of the stranger nights of my life!

CHAPTER SEVEN

IT was a quarter to eleven when Camira climbed the fence the next morning and narrowed her eyes in faint puzzlement as she walked across the paddock and skirted the dam. It all looked very quiet to her for a Saturday morning. Almost as if all the work had been done. In fact the only evidence of any activity was Tim walking his new jumper up and down. Then Marc came round the corner of the shed and she almost bumped into him.

' 'Day, Camira,' he said lightly. 'Feeling tired?'

'No. I slept in. Where is everyone?'

'They've taken the rest of the day off.'

'Do you mean it's all done? Why didn't you tell me? I'd have come earlier. . . .'

'I know,' he agreed. 'Tim!' he called, and waved his arm. 'She's here.'

Tim turned. 'Oh, good,' he called back, and led the horse towards them.

'*Wait* a minute,' said Camira. 'If this is what I think it is!'

'It sure is,' her employer drawled. 'I had to forcibly restrain Tim from coming over at least an hour ago to get you. You're not planning to disappoint him, are you, Camira?'

She set her jaw. 'Him or you?' she queried coldly. 'I told you last night, I'm out of practice and I don't intend to get round like a proper novice for you to have a good laugh at. I. . . .'

'I'd be the last person to laugh, Camira,' Marc said gently. But he added on a barely concealed note of satire, 'Perhaps Thorpe was wrong, though, but he's usually a good judge. Is that why you're reluctant? Or have you lost your nerve? That happens too.'

'I have not lost my nerve,' Camira said flatly, and immediately realised the trap he was leading her so carefully into. She shrugged. '*All right*! I'll take him round.' She turned to Tim who had come up by now. 'I'll have to borrow your hat, Tim. Whoa there, boy!' she said to the tall brown horse, and scratched him gently on his long aristocratic nose. 'What's his name, by the way? And does he still muck up at that particular jump as you were telling me?'

'His name's Cooper's Creek, Camira,' Tim said eagerly, 'but I call him Coop. And he simply refuses it now.'

'Do you now, Coop?' Camira said thoughtfully. 'I wonder why. Give me a leg up, Tim.'

Coop seemed slightly puzzled at the change of rider at first. His brown ears pricked inquisitively as Camira urged him into a walk and he took several playful, skittish, sideways steps, but somewhat tentatively.

Camira said with a gurgle in her voice and an incredible sensation of elation at being back on a horse once more, 'Is that how it is, Coop? You think you might just try me out, do you? Well, I like that because it shows you've got spirit. But nonetheless we're going to walk until I say otherwise, old son. Just like this. That's it!'

They moved off, and she was quite oblivious to the two pairs of intent eyes she left behind. All she was aware of was the feel of the reins held low, the faint creak of the saddle beneath her straight back, the morning air, hot on her arms now, and a certainty that all the birds in this part of the world must be singing.

She walked Coop for a furlong and then brought him to a standstill to adjust the stirrups. He stood patiently enough.

'There,' she said, 'now we can do what you really want to do!' And she urged him into a trot and then a canter and they circled the jumps Tim had so lovingly erected in the middle of the track.

'Ah, yes,' she said to the horse, 'I see the one Tim means. It is a bit formidable, isn't it? Tell you what, we'll try all the others a few times and come back to it a little later.'

Cooper's Creek jumped like a bird, she found with a feeling of sheer exhilaration as she rose in the saddle over his
neck each time he sailed into the air, seemingly quite
effortlessly. She patted his withers when they had completed
the course a second time, the reins in one hand as she
brought him round in a tight turn. 'You're something else,
aren't you?' she said soothingly, and set him towards the
one obstacle they hadn't taken. 'Don't see why you can't
manage it . . . come, here goes!'

They pounded down the green turf towards a set of
double gates, Camira still talking to the horse ready to
gather him and herself over the gates, and Coop gave no
indication of being any other way inclined himself. That
was, until almost the last moment. Then he put the brakes
on and veered sharply and Camira sailed out of the saddle
over his head, over the gate to land on her back on the grass
beyond.

She was still lying there, slightly winded but laughing
softly to herself, when Marc Riley's dark face blotted the
horizon from view and he said crossly, 'What's so damn
funny? Can't you get up?'

'Of course I can get up,' she said, still grinning. 'And I
was laughing at the horse. He's sure got a thing about this
gate. Where is he anyway?' She tried to twist round to see
beyond him, but he was kneeling down beside her and put
his hands on her shoulders.

'Don't worry about the flaming horse. He took off, but
Tim's gone to get him. Here,' he put his arm under her
shoulders and raised her to a sitting position, 'any sprains
or broken bones?'

She shook her head. 'No, really, I'm quite all right. Perhaps a few bruises, but nothing else. You . . . don't have to

hold me,' she added in a voice suddenly gone gruff as she realised his arm was still about her shoulders and she was leaning against him. She looked up sideways at him and surprised an expression of sheer wicked amusement on his face which made her pull away hastily and scramble to her feet. But her legs were unsteady beneath her for a moment and she would have fallen again if he hadn't risen quickly and grabbed her about the waist.

She took a deep breath and resolutely steadied herself, but not before her colour had fluctuated and her heart had started to beat heavily until she was sure Marc must feel it through his hands still holding her waist. She swallowed and wetted her lips and kept her eyes steadfastly on the strong tanned column of his neck as it rose from the open collar of his shirt. However, this wasn't such a good idea either, she discovered, because she was assailed by the sudden incredible longing to slide her hands beneath his shirt and let her fingers trail over his smooth brown shoulders. . . .

It was Tim who came to the rescue, and Camira tore her gaze from a hollow at the base of Marc's neck where a slight pulse-beat was visible, and asked anxiously as Tim came up with Cooper's Creek, 'Is he all right, Tim? He hasn't pulled anything with that bronco exhibition, has he?' and felt the hands about her waist tighten cruelly and then slacken and she was standing alone.

'He's as bright as a button, Camira. The point is, how are you? You came off a beauty!'

'I know,' she agreed with a laugh that got caught in her throat somehow. She went on hurriedly, 'You know, I think I've worked out what it is. I'm sure—either with this gate or one very similar—he must have taken off too long once and come down on it with his back legs.'

Marc straightened up from feeling Cooper's Creek's legs

and said musingly, 'I think you're probably right, Camira. He does have a slight tendency to take off too long. I noticed that the other day. The thing is how to cure him of it. Any ideas?' He looked at her.

'Yes,' she said promptly. 'I think we should re-arrange the jumps so he has a much shorter run-in to this gate. As short as possible and with a sharp turn.' She turned and pointed. 'If you moved that hedge over there, perhaps . . . and this one over here, that should do it. Then, with a bit of luck, he won't have time to even remember his distaste for the gate. Shall we try it?'

'Why not?' said Marc, 'up you go, Tim.'

But Tim hesitated and looked enquiringly at Camira. 'Would you like to? He was jumping beautifully for you just now. That's if you feel up to it.'

'O.K.,' she agreed. 'I'd like to.'

'Well, come on,' Marc said impatiently, 'We can't stand here all day, but watch out. It could be more than a few bruises this time. Up you go! I'll give you a hand with these jumps, Tim.' He turned away, and Camira and Tim exchanged suddenly rueful glances.

'Don't let him rattle you, Camira,' Tim said quietly. 'Remember, it's probably his way of showing concern.'

Or his way of showing his infuriating superiority, Camira thought as she and Coop moved away. 'Whichever it is,' she muttered to the horse, 'we're going to show him this time, mate!'

And show him they did. Twice in fact, and when Camira dismounted she patted the horse and kissed his nose. 'You see, you silly old thing, it was all in your mind.'

Tim was exultant and beaming with gratitude and a boyish desire to please. 'Come and have lunch with us, Camira. Please,' he begged. 'Mrs Leonard said to ask you, ⸏

and besides, I want to ask you . . . well,' he amended, 'we
—that is—oh, do please come!' he ended in a rush.

'I. . . .' Camira temporised, and could think of not one
suitable excuse. 'Well, I. . . .'

'Good,' Tim said firmly. 'Why don't you two go on up
while I put the horse away. I won't be long.' And he strode
away, leaving Camira to the tender mercies of her employer.

Marc said with a perfectly straight face, 'You need to be
a quick thinker when Tim sets his mind to something. Coming?'

Camira sighed. 'I . . . suppose so.' She fell into step beside him. 'What is it he wants to ask me?'

He looked at her meditatively for a long minute. Then he
said, 'I might leave it to him to tell you.'

'Oh, come on!' Camira pleaded. 'The suspense is killing
me.'

'Well, all right. But not until I've got you installed on the
coolest part of the verandah with a long drink.'

He was as good as his word. Which was how Camira came,
some minutes later, to jerk upright from the cane chair she
had sunk into and spill some of Mrs Leonard's homemade
ginger beer into her lap.

'But that's impossible!' she exclaimed angrily. 'You can't
make those kind of arrangements without even consulting
me!'

'I did mention that to Tim,' Marc drawled. 'But after all,
you were instrumental in bringing them together,' he added.

'That doesn't mean . . . just tell me how it all happened
again, will you? It sounds very suspicious to me.'

He said patiently, 'Tim came to me this morning with the
bright idea that we go down to the coast later in the day for
a swim and that he ring up Julie and invite her. I told him it

was fine with me. Then he came back with the news that Julie was going to consult her parents and would ring him back and he'd just had the marvellous idea that if he told her *you* were coming as well, there was no way her parents could refuse just in case they were particularly protective parents—and besides, as he said, it would do Camira the world of good, but she can be hard to persuade, so this might be the best way to do it.'

'To which you agreed, no doubt,' Camira said coldly.

'My exact words were – be it on your own head, Tim.' Marc laughed at her.

'Well, I think you're insufferable!' she said roundly. 'You should have squashed the idea there and then. You. . . .' She turned at the sound of footsteps. It was Tim.

'Has Marc told you?' he said eagerly. 'Don't be cross with me, Camira,' he cajoled, 'it's a perfect day for a swim and once Julie knew you were coming she really went overboard for the idea. Pretty please, Camira!'

This was so much an earnest entreaty, so serious and yet so boyish, Camira felt her heart soften even though she knew his brother was affecting a devilishly, studiously blank face that didn't for one minute hide from her his amusement.

'Well . . .' she hesitated, 'oh, all right, Tim. But next time you should ask first. I might have had something on.' What a lie, she told herself, and as if they don't know it.

But Tim at least endeared himself to her by playing along and saying, solemnly, 'I promise I won't, and thanks a million!'

Camira turned over on the warm sand and sighed contentedly. Tim was quite right. It was a perfect day for the beach, hot and clear but with just a slight breeze to take the sting out of the sun. Before her the long blue and lacy white breakers of the Pacific Ocean rose and fell with a soothing, regular rhythm on to the golden sand and behind and to the left and perhaps a kilometre away, the tall buildings of Surfer's Paradise raised their spires to the blue, blue sky, their windows catching and reflecting brilliantly the rays of the late afternoon sun.

She stretched luxuriously and the figure beside her stirred and sat up.

Marc said as he looked around, 'Where are the kids?'

'In the water.' Camira lifted an arm and pointed to the two frolicking figures. 'They're playing like two young horses,' she said with a grin.

'She seems like a nice kid,' he commented, and lay down again on his side and this time much closer to Camira.

'She is,' she said quietly, and inched a bit away from him.

'Don't worry, Camira,' he said with an amused quirk to his lips and a look she mistrusted completely in his hazel eyes. 'I'm not going to jump on you.'

'I didn't think you were,' she said flatly.

'So why are you as restless as a young filly yourself?'

Because you're altogether too close for comfort, she thought fiercely to herself, and closed her eyes to shut out the sight of his lean, powerful body with its golden tan that had been a source of roughly equal pain and bitter-sweet pleasure to her during the long, hot afternoon. She could still see him, slicing through the surf. . . .

She said. 'Perhaps because I think it's time we went home? It must be nearly five now.'

'But didn't Tim tell you,' he said idly, and brought a hand up to trace the outline of her one-piece bathing suit where it divided over the valley between her breasts, 'our curfew time is not until ten-thirty. I believe he and Julie intend to take in a six o'clock sitting of a movie—some spine-chilling thriller, no doubt ghoulish in the extreme, and to sustain themselves they've expressed a preference for hamburgers and chips and malted milks. I thought,' he added quizzically, 'you might prefer something,' he shrugged and grinned, 'something more in keeping with our age and status.'

Camira blinked and dragged her mind from the utterly lovely sensations his roving fingers were sending through her. Then she pushed his hand away and sat up. 'You planned this,' she said tautly, accusingly. 'But for once you've outsmarted yourself, *mate*! Because even in Surfer's I doubt if my tatty shorts and T-shirt, which is all I've got to wear, will gain me entry to anything better than a milk-bar.'

Marc rolled over on to his back and squinted up at her. 'That's no problem. The family owns a unit down here. We all have a key and I happen to know no one is in residence at the moment. See over there, Camira?' She followed the line of his arm towards one of the tallest buildings etched against the skyline.

'Do you mean. . . .' she began uncertainly.

'Yes,' he said, 'one of the top ones. 'My father and Tim's mother are its most frequent inhabitants, when they're not travelling around the world. That's why I bought Camira Lodge. It's so handy. And what's more, there's a Chinese restaurant in the building.' He sat up suddenly. 'Do you like braised beef in black bean sauce and sweet and sour duck, or perhaps chicken and cashews? I can vouch for the quality of their food. In a word it's superb.'

Camina was terribly tempted for a moment, not even so much by the thought of the foods he had mentioned but by the warmth of his personality, by his vitality and by the thought of his quick, sometimes cutting, always alert brain. It was impossible to be bored in Marc Riley's company, she thought with a stifled feeling of—was it almost longing? Yes, it was. But that's the crux of the whole matter isn't it, Camira? she told herself. You might not get bored with him, whereas he's bound to get bored with you . . . think of Lisa. . . .

But the decision was wrested from her and for one short instant she pondered Tim's motives as he and Julie threw themselves down in the sand at their feet. 'I'm starving,' Tim proclaimed loudly. 'Just starving!'

'Well,' Marc said reasonably, 'I reckon the answer is to pick up your and Julie's chosen fare on the way to the unit and you can munch it while you get changed for the movies. How does that sound?'

'Great!' said Tim. 'Just great.' He rolled over and added ingenuously, 'Sure you don't want to come to the movies with us, you two?'

The unit was the last word in luxury, knee-deep from wall to wall in pure white shaggy carpet with metallic blue and silver wallpaper in the lounge and a matching blue and white lounge suite covered in a rough, heavy-textured linen. The lounge led to a roof garden complete with gently waving palm trees and a swimming pool.

Camira sighed desolately as she took it all in. Was it any wonder the Lisas of this world were continually uneasy and on guard? Who could blame them? Only me, she thought sadly. And only me probably because I know what this kind of affluence can lead to. Heartbreak. And just how am I going to get through the rest of this evening? she asked herself despairingly. If ever anyone was set up, it's you, Camira Johnston. But Tim—surely he wouldn't do that to me . . .?

She stood in the middle of the lounge. Julie and Tim were showering and Marc was moving around in the kitchen, unwrapping the hamburgers they'd stopped to buy.

'Thirsty, Camira?' he called.

She came out of her reverie. 'Yes, thank you.'

'Here.' He came through into the lounge and handed her a frosted glass. 'Hurry up, you two,' he called, then turned back to her. 'Why don't you take your drink on to the terrace? I'm going to run Tim and Julie to the theatre as soon as they've eaten and I'll organise our own meal, and while I'm out you can have a shower if you'd like to.'

She nodded somewhat like a sleepwalker and his keen gaze rested on her thoughtfully.

'Why so pensive?' he queried. 'You're not planning to run out on me, are you, by any chance? And try to hitch-hike home? You wouldn't be so foolish, would you now?'

'No . . . no,' she said slowly, and turned away.

The bathroom was the most luxurious she had ever seen, with a sunken marble bath, gold wallpaper and jade-green carpeting and one entire wall of mirror panelling. She examined herself carefully as she stepped out of the shower and had to admit that the sea and the sun had not done her any harm. They'd added a pleasant glow, in fact.

She dried her hair vigorously with a fluffy rose-pink towel and then having been commanded by her employer to make full use of everything in the bathroom which was all there specifically for the use of guests, she donned her under-clothes and a short, sleeveless towelling robe that matched the bath towels exactly, then took up the blow-dryer hanging from its own special clip on the wall and completed the task of drying her long hair. She had also made use of the delicately perfumed body lotion in a beautiful crystal decanter and patted some of the matching perfumed talc from a crystal bowl on to her body with an enormous jade swansdown puff.

She still had the blow-dryer in one hand and was combing her hair with the other, admiring the way it billowed out in a shower of beige silk around her shoulders when one of the mirror panels opened before her startled gaze and Marc stepped into the bathroom.

She clicked the dryer off and swung round to look at the door set in the opposite wall. The door she had locked so carefully when she had come in, and she swung back to say irately, 'I should have guessed!'

'Guessed what?' he drawled. 'That my father has a peculiar sense of humour? That he had that door put in so he could surprise my mother in her bath? I don't think she objected,' he said casually as he set two brimming wine glasses down on the marble counter. 'They're very close, my . . . our parents, despite the fact that he's in his sixties and she's in her late forties.'

'What's that got to do with it?' Camira asked. 'I'm very happy for them, but I thought this was the guest bathroom. Surely if they're so happy. . . .'

'It is now,' he interjected smoothly, and took the comb from her fingers and drew it idly through her hair. 'And that door has a lock on it on the other side since they rearranged things. Matter of fact, I only remembered where the key was hidden after I'd knocked on the other door and realised you couldn't hear me through the dryer. The sun's setting now and the view from the terrace is quite spectacular. It'd be such a pity to miss it . . . your hair is beautiful,' he added softly as he wound it round his fingers and coiled it at the base of her throat. 'But I think I've already told you that, haven't I?'

'Yes,' she said, and was frankly terrified by the husky note in her voice. She drew a deep breath and said more steadily. 'I'll just get dressed, then, and I'll join you on the terrace.'

'You are dressed,' said Marc with a quizzically raised eyebrow, 'and very becomingly. Come.' He slid his knuckles down towards her bosom, but when she tensed immediately, he lifted his hand away and caught one of her own with it. 'You take your glass and I'll take mine,' he murmured, and led her through the conventional doorway and out through to the terrace, where the sunset was every bit as spectacular as he had predicted.

They stayed on the terrace, not talking but idly sipping the chilled white wine until the last rays of light had left the ocean and the broad sweep of the Nerang river behind them was only a faint gleam in the dusk and everywhere, save for the expanse of the ocean, pinpricks of light were springing up to pierce the gathering night and turn Surfer's Paradise into a fairy-tale city.

The doorbell chimed musically and Marc turned to her and said, 'That'll be the food. Shall we eat inside? It's a bit breezy now, isn't it?'

She nodded.

'Good,' he said, and pointed to an alcove in the lounge that held a blue-painted cane table and two chairs. 'Would you mind setting the table for me? Everything should be in the cupboard set into the wall.'

Camira crossed to the alcove obediently and pulled open the cupboard. She chose a dusky pink linen tablecloth to cover the glass-topped table and an assortment of cutlery, but she returned these when she came across two pairs of ivory chopsticks. Then she chose several dishes from the magnificent and obviously valuable dinner service and set them on the table.

A sound behind her made her turn, to see Marc wheeling a trolley towards her that incorporated a special heating section, and upon this, with their lids off and emitting from their slightly steaming contents the most delicious, mouth-watering aromas, were set a series of bowls. And next to them in an austere silver bucket stood a bottle of champagne.

She said stupidly as he put the bucket on the table, 'What are we celebrating?'

He grinned at her. 'Nothing. Yet. It was all I could find in the wine rack. Why don't you sit down, Camira, and serve yourself. I'll just put some music on.'

Camira made a conscious effort through the duration of that meal to act as normally as she could. She introduced the subject of Tim's horses as a topic of conversation and managed to keep it alive for a good twenty minutes. Then she switched to the subject of horses in general and Camira Lodge's forthcoming debut as a training establishment once more. They touched on Mission Beach, the horse which had stood on her foot and his peculiar lack of form, which had turned out to be caused by a virus. And this discussion lasted another good twenty or thirty minutes and to the end of the meal, but it petered out finally and Camira was aghast to realise that it was only eight o'clock and that Marc was sitting back in his chair with his hazel eyes resting on her and an expression of ironical expectancy in them.

She bit her lip. 'What about Tim and Julie?' she asked nervously. 'What time does their movie come out?'

He shrugged. 'In about half an hour. But I said I'd pick them up outside that new pancake manor, whatever they call it. They're going to treat themselves to strawberry and ice-cream waffles. I said we'd be there about nine-thirty. That will give us plenty of time to get home by ten-thirty.'

'Oh,' was all she could find to say.

He grinned faintly. 'No more scintillating conversation?' he queried. Then, 'Maybe you're right, we have discussed horses pretty thoroughly. One could almost say exhaustively.' He grimaced and rested an elbow on the table and leant across to refill her glass. 'Tell me, is that all you and David Thorpe talked about when you were engaged?'

Camira took a sharp breath. 'I suppose he told you,' she said bitterly.

Marc lounged back and let his eyes roam over her in a way that made her heart suddenly race. 'He didn't have to. I'm not blind, nor am I stupid. And if he hadn't given himself away, the attitudes of all your friends, especially Jane Sinclair, would have made me very curious, to say the least.'

She raised her eyes suddenly. 'Well, now you know,' she said, attempting to be casual. 'If I'd known he was a friend of yours, I'd never have told you.'

'Oh, he is—that,' he murmured in agreement. 'Or rather, put it this way—I've known him for years. We both represented Australia in the World Cup once. From a man's point of view he's what you call a good bloke.'

She lifted her shoulders in a tiny gesture as if disclaiming much interest. 'He could be. I wouldn't know.'

Marc went on, 'But from a lady's point of view . . . ah well, I should say he was a lot more. I should say he was little less than sensational. If you could count the numbers of them that flocked around him as any kind of a guide.'

'So what?' Camira said flatly.

He laughed softly at her. 'You did that very well, my dear. But I must admit there is one thing that puzzles me.'

She sighed. 'What?' she asked wearily.

'Well, it's like this,' he said patiently. 'David's a very experienced man, and if you got as far as getting engaged to him, something must have gone horribly amiss with his technique for him to have to go the lengths he apparently did to get you to go to bed with him.'

'Perhaps it's just that I'm some kind of a freak,' she said evenly. 'Perhaps, when he thought he was marrying Camira Lodge too, it didn't seem so important to him.'

'Or perhaps you haven't been quite open with me, Camira,' Marc said slowly. 'I could have bought your theory, if I hadn't seen the way he looked at you. But having seen it, I know damned well that he's not indifferent to you, and I doubt if he ever was. I've never seen quite that degree of intensity about David Thorpe. And it had nothing whatsoever to do with the Lodge.'

She didn't say anything for a while but stared unseeingly at her empty plate, marshalling her thoughts and feelings. Finally she looked at him and said painfully, 'I'm not sure I understand you. But it doesn't really matter, does it? I mean,' she closed her eyes briefly, 'what *does* it matter whether you think I slept with David or not? I. . . .'

'Oh, it matters—to a degree. Not so much the act itself, although that . . . well,' Marc shrugged, 'but I would rather you were truthful with me, because I don't think any other way would be the right way to start off a marriage.'

'A . . . *what* did you say?' Camira asked faintly.

'I think you heard,' he commented dryly. 'I'd like to marry you, Camira. I think I was attracted to you from the moment you first offered to hit me. I might not have realised it quite then, but I certainly knew it when I came over to see you that night and found you sitting in a pool of lamplight like a. . . .'

Camira stumbled to her feet. 'Stop it!' she stormed. 'This is just a . . . *mockery*! In one breath you tell me you don't believe a word I say and in the next you talk about marriage and being attracted to me. Your trouble is you're attracted to every passable girl who comes your way and your next problem is that you've got far too much money to be good for you! Well, I knew that before I saw all this,' she gestured contemptuously around the luxurious room.'

'I don't see the logic of that,' he retorted cuttingly. 'What the bloody hell has that got to do with marrying you?'

'I'll tell you,' she said fiercely. 'For once, you realised it might be a little harder to get what you wanted . . . from me, possibly after I told you all that *nonsense* about me and David, but you couldn't bear to be thwarted, could you? And for a rich man the next step comes very easily, doesn't it? Marry in haste and repent not at all. *All* it takes is a generous divorce settlement and the thing is done! But I'm not at all dazzled by. . . .'

'So it was nonsense,' he interrupted acutely as he stared up at her. 'You did sleep with David Thorpe, but when you found out he wasn't going to go through with the wedding, you knocked him back? Is that why he looks at you like some thirst-crazed traveller who's strayed off the Birdsville Track?'

'Look,' she spat at him, 'I *meant* I should never have told you anything, let along try to explain any of the undercurrents of the whole miserable business, because it's only set your fertile imagination going.'

'You could prove it, you know,' he drawled at her, and she saw that hateful smile lurking in his eyes again.

'How?' she demanded. 'Do you really think I would sleep with you to prove my honesty and integrity? To prove that I hadn't slept with David? Or anyone else. Is what you think?' she asked contemptuously.

Marc stood up. 'I did wonder if you might sleep with me because you wanted to,' he said quietly.

'*Wanted* to?'

'Yes, wanted to.' He grinned suddenly as she retreated a step. 'Or is it sunstroke that causes you to blush like this, Camira? And what is it that causes your heart to beat like a train? Because I'll lay you London to a brick on it is right now.' And so saying he reached almost lazily for her, but there was nothing lazy about the way he caught her wrists with one hand or the way the other hand pulled the sash of the rose-pink towelling robe open with a flick.

He laid his hand lightly over her heart. 'I thought so,' he said with a wry smile. 'I felt it yesterday when you fell off that damned horse. Long after it should have returned to normal. It made me wonder then. Perhaps this will ease it?'

He bent his head and gravely kissed her on the lips with his one hand still on her heart and his other hand locked around her wrist.

Camira stood as if turned to stone as his warm lips lingered on hers. It was a very gentle, sedate kiss, but it sent the most incredible sensations racing through her whole body that quite obliterated any thought of escape from her mind. She didn't respond, but she couldn't prevent a deep shudder from shaking her from head to foot.

Marc lifted his head and they stood captured as if in a bubble of time, staring deep into each other's eyes. Then he dropped both his hands and Camira instinctively knew that now was the time to retreat. That if she didn't, she'd be making the most appalling mistake. But her limbs refused to move and she could only to continue to look up into his eyes as if she was drowning in their dark depths, with her lips slightly parted now and her breathing accelerated.

And then it was too late. She'd had her chance and she hadn't taken it. Marc reached for her again, slowly and deliberately, his hands sliding beneath her arms and round to her back and down to her waist and the curve of her hips, and at the same drawing her forward to cradle her softness against the hard, powerful length of him. At first it was a delicate embrace, his hands moving up and down her back and her hips, slowly, lingeringly but soon an urgency crept into it and he was moulding her to him so that she felt the strength of his thighs against her own and her hands came up, involuntarily it seemed, to rest just her fingertips on his broad shoulders as she'd wanted to do several times, she knew.

His eyes never left her upturned face, her parted lips, and he lowered his head to meet them with his own almost in slow motion. And at the last moment she knew that this would be no gentle salute, no chaste touching of his mouth to hers—but the thought was blotted from her mind almost as soon as it was born by a fierce, intense longing as his lips came down punishingly, brutally on hers.

When he raised his head at last Camira saw the beautiful lamplit room whirl around her and knew she would have fallen but for his arms still about her, and she didn't demur when he picked her up and carried her to the wide, soft, linen-covered settee. She didn't demur when she felt his weight on the broad cushions beside her. She even forgot herself so far as to turn towards him and make no protests when he slid the towelling robe off her shoulders and started to kiss her again, slowly and exquisitely down the slender column of her neck, to linger at the base of her throat while he pushed her bra-strap aside, and a fine trembling seemed to break out along her smooth skin as his mouth moved ever downwards and her breasts swelled and their peaks hardened in joyful anticipation.

With a soundless groan, she cradled his dark head to her

and allowed herself the unbelievable luxury of running her fingers through his thick hair, and she shivered in ecstasy as she felt him run one hand down the bare expanse of her thigh.

Then she gently put her hands on his shoulders and pushed him away. For a long moment they lay side by side, not touching but each catching their breath. She sat up first and then gathered the robe about her.

Her eyes jerked to Marc's face as he said softly, wryly, 'Is this what I think it is, Camira?'

She closed her eyes briefly and looked away resolutely.

He sat up too and she stumbled to her feet as if to flee, but he caught at the hem of her robe. '*Tell* me, Camira,' he said insistently.

She took a deep breath and turned back. He let go of the hem and sprawled back on the cushions. She shivered again at the expression in his eyes—a bleak look of contempt almost.

She said haltingly, 'I'm not . . . I mean, it was as much me then as you. I'm not. . . .'

'Blaming me?' he supplied. 'You're very generous, Camira.'

'No!' She bit her lip and sought desperately for the right words. 'I'm not denying that I responded in a way that led you to think . . . to think. . . .'

'Go on,' he said curtly. 'I get your drift.' He straightened up impatiently. 'In fact what you're trying to tell me is this, isn't it? You responded to some primitive physical force over which you had no control—for a time—that anyone else being so minded could have evoked from you? Is that what you're trying to say in a roundabout way?'

She flinched but said honestly, 'Not anyone. You. But that doesn't guarantee that it still isn't—wasn't—a kind of lust. I don't . . . love you any more than you really love me.'

'Do you always separate lust and love, Camira? Put them in neat little compartments with neat little labels? And as a matter of interest, where does my offer of marriage fit into your filing system? As a slightly inexplicable quirk of a man with too much money for his own good? Is that what you *really* think?'

She whispered, 'I don't really know what to think. But just last night I saw you with another girl in your arms. I saw you . . . holding her, dancing with her . . . as if you were making love to her.'

'And I saw someone, mentally anyway, making love to you, whenever his eyes rested on you. Which was an awful lot of the time, my dear innocent Camira. Are you trying to tell me you're jealous of Lisa?'

'No!' she said hotly. 'That's as ridiculous as you expecting me to believe you were jealous of David.'

Marc stood up and swore suddenly. 'There's one thing about you, Camira,' he said coldly, 'that I don't like. And that's your absolute certainty that you can read my mind, and everyone else's for that matter. And that utter certainty carries you through to the point where you're determined to ignore the evidence of your own body, to reduce everything we just shared in this room and on this couch to the level of a cheap thrill. You haven't got the courage to take those lovely sensations and explore them and let them grow and perhaps even be surprised at what could come out of them, because you're firmly convinced, on the very limited knowledge of my one relationship you've blundered into with one woman, that I'm a rake of the lowest order.'

'Might not Lisa be tempted to think something like that if she blundered in here now?'

'Lisa, my dear, would try to annihiliate you in her own

inimitable bitchy manner, but for all that she can be a bitch of the highest order, there's one thing you can't but help admire her for. She knows what she wants, she's not afraid to admit it to herself. She's not so scared of living and breathing and feeling that she walls herself up in an ivory tower. And if she cops a knock from life, she picks herself up and goes again. A far cry from your passive, gutless way of doing things,' Marc finished contemptuously.

Camira stood with her fists clenched and gasped as a wave of anger flooded her. 'If that's the case, why don't you ask *her* to marry you? I'm sure she'd jump at it.'

'I might just do that,' he said with the old mockery, and glanced at his watch. 'You'd better get some clothes on. There's no point in staying here any longer.'

She swung on her heel, still shaking with pent-up emotion, and blundered into a small, solid table as she dashed furiously at the tears that had sprung to her eyes. Tears of rage, tears of hurt as she peered down at her shin to see a bruise already forming. But if anything this seemed to make Marc more sardonic. He came up behind her and turned her round impatiently. 'Your clothes are that way,' he said cruelly, and pointed in the direction of the bathroom. 'And it's too late for tears now, Camira. Save 'em for the day you wake to yourself and start to wonder whether you just might have misjudged me. Save 'em for the day when you realise that love and lust are inextricably bound together and then you'll know what we do to each other is something special, something you might never find again. But it will be too late then, Camira. Much too late.'

Too late . . . much too late! Camira sat up in bed and held her head in her hands. Those words had even managed to penetrate her dreams like an unsteady refrain. What if he

was right? Oh, but it's such an old argument! David used
it on you three years ago. . . .

But you didn't feel quite the same about David, did you,
Camira? she reminded herself. You certainly never allowed
yourself to do what you did this evening. Never really had
to battle with yourself like this.

'I got engaged to him, though, didn't I?' she said out
aloud. 'I must have felt something! How come it's just disappeared as if it never existed? How come?' she asked herself torturedly.

'How come?' she found herself repeating the question to
Jane the following evening after an exhausting, backbreak-
ing day tending her stall. 'Now, when I see him again,' she
went on, 'I just can't imagine how I got myself engaged to
him. Do you remember me in those days, Jane?'

'I remember,' Jane said thoughtfully. 'I was engaged to
Alan. Your mother, for some strange reason I'll never understand, was resisting you every inch of the way when you
naturally wanted to progress beyond the pony-club stage. I
particularly remember one magnificent row you had when
you desperately wanted to compete at the Brisbane Show—
the Ekka—and she just wouldn't hear of it.'

She swirled her cup of coffee in her hand and added. 'To
be quite candid, I always thought David Thorpe represented
a chance to break free of your mother's stranglehold. She
. . . I don't know, but over those last two years, there was
something almost demented about her. Her beaut personality—and it was beaut before then—just sort of crumbled,
somehow. Under pressure, I suppose. I mean, it's very easy
to sit here and be critical, but,' she lifted her eyes to Camira's
face. 'I don't think you ever fell in love with David Thorpe.
Not the way I fell for Alan. I think it was circumstance that

pushed you into it. You know, when you're only eighteen, you're not the wisest of creatures, or else why wouldn't we all be put on this earth knowing everything? And to be perfectly honest, although no one in their right minds would have welcomed the way it happened, I couldn't help feeling relieved that you saw him in his true colours.'

'She . . . Grandpapa told me why she would never allow me to compete,' Camira said unsteadily. 'Her brother—one of her brothers—was killed in a fall. I'll never understand why she didn't tell me herself.'

'And your father never mentioned it?' Jane asked.

'No. That was part of the power she had over him. She must have forbidden him to say anything about it.'

Jane said helplessly, 'Camira, there are people like that. Headstrong, full of nervous energy, who mean well but can't quite control their impulses. It's inherent and I think they fight their own peculiar battle all their lives. Don't be bitter towards her if you can help it. But I think you're right to feel,' she shrugged, 'a distaste for someone who tried to capitalise on the situation. And above all, forget trying to diagnose all the whys and the wherefores. Don't dwell on the past. Leave it be,' she said gently, 'because it's only the future that counts, believe me, love.'

And for some reason, Jane's loving and sane advice finally broke Camira's reserve and she sobbed wholeheartedly into her friend's shoulder for several minutes.

'There,' Jane said finally, 'doesn't that feel better? Hey, I'm supposed to be the tearful one, remember? But,' she added seriously, 'this bout of tears is a long time overdue, love.'

'I guess so,' Camira admitted, and sniffed. 'I suppose the party and David appearing out of the blue, brought it all back.'

'Sure,' her best friend said wisely. 'Sure. Unless there's something else you'd like to tell me?'

'What else could there be?' Camira gulped. 'Surely that's enough?'

'Oh, plenty,' Jane said hastily. Well, it's a start anyway, she added to herself.

CHAPTER EIGHT

'I could go a cold one, son!' Bob sang surprisingly tunefully and wiped his face with one grimy forearm. 'Phew! It's hot! How come you always manage to look so cool, calm and collected, Camira?'

'I was just wondering the same thing myself,' Tim agreed as he threw himself down on a bale of hay. He sat up almost immediately and looked around warily.

Bob chuckled. 'It's okay, he's gone up to the house. I reckon with a bit of luck we might not see too much of him again today. There,' he squinted through the open shed doorway as a car roared down the driveway and turned through the double gates on to the road, 'what did I tell ya?' He pulled open a small refrigerator and drew out a cold can of beer. 'Want one, Camira?'

'I'll have a soft drink, Bob.'

'Me too,' said Tim. He looked round again. 'Hey, Marty! It's safe to come out, mate! Wherever you're hiding yourself. The boss has—in a word—gone walkabout.'

'And not a minute too soon, if you ask me,' Marty said

gloomily as he emerged from the harness room where he'd been polishing bridles. 'You know, I honestly wish he'd bawl us all out and get it off his chest. This orgy of work is enough to kill yer in this heat! I mean, I've been in some fussy stables, but this is laughable,' he said aggrievedly. 'The damn floor is so clean now you could eat off it. As I should know, having been chief and only scrubber,' he said pointedly.

'Well, the rest of us ain't been exactly idle,' Bob said briefly. 'And ya gotta admit, he worked as hard as we did. What I want to know is what brought it all on. He was as bright as a button on Saturday—didn't he even take you swimming? You two?'

'Yes,' Tim and Camira said in unison.

'Matter of fact,' Tim went on, 'it was a terrific day, wasn't it, Camira? He couldn't have been nicer!'

Camira felt her muscles relax slightly. So Tim hadn't noticed that the day had ended on a very different note. . . . She swallowed as she heard him say,

'Know what I reckon it is, don't you, Bob?'

'Yep.' Bob drained his can and reached into the fridge for another. 'It's that crazy sheila.' He imitated Lisa Mackenzie's high-pitched voice. 'What a delightful coincidence, darling!'

Tim and Marty laughed.

Bob went on, 'Coincidence my foot! I reckon as soon as the bush telegraph started to buzz with the news of a party here on Camira, she pricked up her little pointed ears and went straight to work. And why you didn't punch her on the nose for what she said to you, Camira, I can't imagine!'

They all laughed at this until finally Camira said more soberly, 'I must admit the thought did cross my mind.'

'You did the right thing, Camira,' Tim said stoutly. 'You

made her look so small.'

Camira shivered suddenly and thought, maybe to you, Tim, but not to your brother. She stood up and stretched. 'I think I'll hie me off home, fellers. I've been neglecting my garden lately and the weeds are flourishing.'

'I'll hook the tractor up to the trailer and bring you a load of manure,' Bob said obligingly. 'I reckon the trailer's about full.'

'Thanks, Bob,' she said gratefully, and turned to go. But Tim called her back.

'Going to come over and jump with me this afternoon when it's cooler?'

Camira pretended to consider for a moment, although she had no intention of spending a minute more at Camira Lodge than she absolutely had to. She said at last, regretfully, 'I'm really so behind, Tim, it's going to take me a little time to catch up. But when I do I'll let you know.'

'All right,' he said with good-natured resignation. 'I might ring Julie up, then. I've offered to teach her to ride.'

And this was to be the pattern of Camira's days for the next fortnight. She worked herself to the point where she was too exhausted to think and her garden bloomed and her vegetables produced better than they ever had. Plump, red, juicy, tomatoes, silver-beet that was almost awesome in the size of its dark green crinkled leaves. Chokoes that melted in the mouth when boiled and served with butter. Golden corn that she just couldn't grow fast enough for the demand in the district, let alone for her Sunday stall.

And all the time Marc treated her with a polite, impersonal distance after that one day of furious industry he had exposed his whole staff to, as if he were totally indifferent to her and had never been otherwise.

David Thorpe came to see her about ten days after the party, but she had simply refused to be drawn into any kind of discussion or confrontation and for the whole half-hour he'd spent with her she'd gone on pruning the creepers that were threatening to smother her verandah until he'd grabbed the shears from her and chucked them over the rail in a rage. But she had only shrugged and walked inside, locking the screen door behind her and leaving him to drive off with a squeal of tyres and a racing engine.

Jane and Alan had taken some time off and gone up-country with the twins to visit Jane's parents, so the only human contact Camira had for that fortnight was her daily stint at the stables and the strangers she served in her stall at the weekends. She often saw Tim and Julie in the distance across the fence, Tim mounted on Cooper's Creek and Julie on a much quieter horse on a leading rein, and she was surprised at how desperately she wished they would come to call on her, but she knew it was her fault that they did not. Tim had invited her over to ride several times since she had first refused him, but she had been so definite that she was far too busy, he had finally taken the hint with just a tinge of hurt in his eyes that had cut her to the quick.

Another source of pain had come from Marc himself. She noted with surprise one morning that the jumps had been cleared from the middle of the track and two polo goalposts had been erected, and from then on she was subjected each morning to the sight of him exercising his polo ponies with Tim's eager assistance. It was a special form of torture to see his lean powerful body tall in the saddle, to see the strength of his shoulders as he swung his arm to hit the puck, to see the grace and beauty of his supple movements.

But she steadfastly refused to allow her misery to take hold until Bob said to her again, 'You got me beat, Camira!

You work like a damned slave day and night and every day I expect you to break down like a horse that's been flattened, but you pop up like a daisy! All the same,' he ventured as he looked at her closely and took in the faint violet shadows beneath her eyes, 'you want to be sure you don't overdo it.' He put his head to one side. 'Sure you're eating properly? You look a bit tuckered up to me, if you know what I mean.'

She laughed. 'I thought it was only horses who looked tuckered up, Bob. I don't think I'm flattered.'

'You wasn't meant to be,' he said seriously. 'I reckon you should ease up, kid. You're getting to look real fine-drawn. Can't think why it took me so long to notice,' he muttered. 'You take my advice and ease up!'

She didn't take his advice and no one regretted it more bitterly than she did when a couple of mornings later she reached for a towel to dry down a horse she had just washed, but instead of picking the towel up, she groped for the railing to support herself as the concrete shed floor seemed to move alarmingly beneath her feet and she crumpled up in a dead faint at her employer's feet.

She came to to find herself lying on something soft but unwilling to open her eyes in case the world was still behaving so peculiarly and to hear Bob and Marc conversing close at hand.

'I warned her,' Bob said. 'Only the other day. It's just too much for a slip of a sheila,' he added angrily. 'You seen the size of the plot she works single-handed? I tell you, the kid never stops! I'm surprised you ain't noticed she's been looking peaky yourself. If she was a horse you'da picked it up soon enough.'

'My . . . expertise obviously doesn't extend to the human female. And she's free, white and twenty-one, as the saying goes. She doesn't have to work herself to death.' Marc sounded impatient.

'On the other hand,' Bob pointed out coldly, 'you're quite happy to accept that she's one of the best, hardest working flaming strappers you've ever had, and all for a trickle of water!'

'Just listen to me, Bob Duffy,' her employer ground out, 'she's also one of the stubbornest sheilas you're ever likely to meet, and she wouldn't be slaving for a mere trickle of water if I wasn't quite convinced anything more I offered her would be hurled right back at me *plus* whatever else happened to be at hand.'

Surprisingly, Bob chuckled then. 'Well, that must make a change for you,' he said genially. 'All the other sheilas you mix with are quite the opposite, ain't they? Still, we all live and learn, don't we?'

'You're so right, mate. And seeing as you're such a fount of absolute wisdom perhaps you'd bend your mind to the problem of what to do with her now? Mrs Leonard's taking a couple of days off, in case *you* hadn't noticed.'

'Oh, I noticed,' Bob said irrepressibly. 'And I tell you something, I'm not altogether sorry. I need a breathing space from that strong-minded lady—in case *you* hadn't noticed. What about her friends? Camira's?' he asked.

'Well, the Sinclairs are away, I know, because I went down to see 'em the other night.'

'Hmmm,' Bob said judiciously. 'Tell you what. I bet you London to a brick on all she needs is a few days' rest and some good tucker. Now I happen to know because Tim was only telling me the other day, your folks are in Tahiti or somewhere Godforsaken like that, so that fancy unit at Surfer's is lying empty. Take her down there for a few days. . . .'

'No!' Camira's eyes fluttered open. 'No,' she said shakily. 'I'm all right. At least,' she amended as she tried to sit up but found she couldn't quite make it, 'I will be, I know. It's just that it's so hot. . . .'

Under any other circumstances she would have found it quite comical to see the surprise and similar expressions of irritation in the two pairs of eyes now turned towards her.

'You're not and you know it,' Marc Riley said abruptly. 'And what Bob says makes sense. Don't worry, you can have the unit to yourself apart from the cleaning lady, who I'm sure would be delighted to see you get some decent food into yourself.'

'But my garden!'

'Blow your garden,' Bob said equally abruptly. 'Anyway, me and Marty and Tim can keep an eye on it for you.'

'But. . . .'

'But nothing, Camira,' Marc said roughly. 'You have only one alternative, and that is to stay right here in my bedroom where I can keep an eye on you.'

'Good,' Bob said approvingly, 'that's how you got to handle 'em. Like a spirited filly. You gotta make sure they know who's boss.'

'Oh, Bob,' she sighed despairingly, but with a laugh she couldn't prevent from catching in her throat. And then the laugh inexplicably turned to tears.

Camira stood in the middle of the blue and silver and white room and wondered at fate. She'd been so sure she'd never see this room again.

She turned at a sound behind her. Marc dropped her bag to the floor.

He said, 'I've put the groceries in the kitchen. The pantry's pretty well stocked with tinned stuff, but you should eat as much fresh food as you can. The cleaning lady is going to come in every day while you're here and she won't mind doing some shopping for you.'

'Thank you,' she said uncertainly.

He raised his eyebrows and shrugged. 'It's nothing,' he said casually. 'How do you feel now?'

'Fine.'

'Well, you don't look it. You're still as pale as a ghost and you look as if a good wind would blow you away. Hell,' he said unemotionally, 'I should have kept you home as I threatened.'

'You should have let me go home to my own home,' she said tiredly. 'Which bedroom should I use?'

'The guest bedroom is the last one at the end of the passageway. Here, this is a spare set of keys in case you feel like going down to the beach. But the pool's there—when you feel strong enough.' He dug into his trouser pocket and withdrew a fifty-dollar note. 'I don't how you're off for cash, but in case you need anything, I'll leave you this.' He put the bill on the small table she'd stumbled over and weighted it down with an ashtray.

Camira raised her eyes to him.

'You can pay me back some time,' he said shortly. He looked around. 'I think that's it. I'll give you a ring to-morrow to see how you are, but my advice to you now is to make yourself a light supper and then go to bed. Goodnight, Camira.'

She stared blindly across the room. She heard the front door open and close and she clenched her fists and gritted her teeth, but it was an unequal struggle. She sank down on to the settee and sobbed distractedly.

She never knew how long it was before she realised she was not alone. But some sixth sense seemed to claim her and she lifted her tear-streaked face from her hands to stare incredulously at the tall figure before her.

'I . . . I didn't hear you come back,' she said desperately, and scrubbed at her brimming eyes with her wrists.

'No,' he said sombrely, 'you wouldn't have. You do see that I can't leave you like this, don't you, Camira?'

'I . . . I . . . oh, God!'

'I know. You wish you'd never met me. I'm conscious of the same sentiment, believe me.' He crossed to the bar and splashed some brandy into a glass. 'Drink this,' he said on a gentler note. 'Better still, bring it with you.' He picked up her case. 'And please—don't argue for once.'

Camira lay in the huge bed feeling drowsy and supremely comfortable. She took another sip of brandy and felt its warmth slide down. If this is the spare room, she mused idly, I just wonder what the master bedroom is like? And to add to the luxury of the room an air-conditioner—somewhere hidden from view—purred silently and maintained an even, cool temperature.

She felt her eyes close. I'm so tired, she thought. Too tired to. . . . But her eyes flicked open and she struggled to a sitting positition as Marc put a tray down beside the bed.

'You shouldn't have,' she protested.

'Why not?' he said offhandedly. He sat down on the side of the bed. 'It's only some soup and a fresh, warm roll. Do you think you can manage it?'

'I . . . yes,' she said uncomfortably. 'Thank you,' she added as he placed a pillow on her knees and put the tray on it carefully. He handed her a linen napkin.

'That's better,' he observed as she drank the soup. 'You don't look quite so wan.'

'I feel a real fraud! I wish you wouldn't wait on me like

this.' I wish you'd go away too, she added to herself conscious of her thin, plain cotton nightgown.

He said, 'From tomorrow, I won't. We usually eat most of our meals out on the terrace when we're here. Provided it's not too breezy.'

She said with the soup spoon poised halfway to her mouth, 'You're not spending tomorrow here too!'

Marc shrugged. 'And the next day. And the next. They're racing at the Gold Coast on Saturday, so it's quite handy really. You might even feel like coming to the races.'

'But what about the Lodge? How will they cope with both of us away?' she demanded.

'They'll cope for a few days. As a matter of fact Bob's a very good coper and he likes nothing better than to be left on his own occasionally.' Marc grinned. 'I don't suffer from the delusion that I'm indispensable.'

'And *what* will they think?' she asked with ominous calm.

'They can think what they like. But as a matter of fact they're a pretty nice bunch of people who don't normally go jumping to wild conclusions. Besides,' he stood up and picked up the tray, 'have you finished? Good, we both know there'll be nothing to think about, don't we, Camira? *Look*,' he added evenly. 'I think we all feel guilty about you, one way or another, and we all want to help. This is the best way to do it. It's as simple as that. Now try and sleep if you can, and if you want anything, don't hesitate. I'll be just down the passageway.' He went out without a backward glance.

The surprising thing was that she slept, slept deeply and dreamlessly for hours and hours, about twelve hours straight, in fact, and it was nine o'clock, she saw, when she finally woke the next morning. She stretched lazily and jerked upright to stare at the pattern of sunlight that fell across the richly quilted bedcover. Her hand flew to her mouth as she recalled the events of the previous day.

'Now look what you've done, Camira,' she said out aloud. 'Just how . . . how can you handle *this*?'

But during that long leisurely day 'this', she discovered, required no handling on her part at all. Marc was polite, still concerned for her health, and when she relaxed after the first few tense hours, was good company.

They lazed in the sun for most of the morning and he swam in the sparkling aquamarine pool, but he wouldn't allow her to more than cool off in the shallows and after a delicious lunch prepared for them by the versatile cleaning lady, who far from being surprised or shocked seemed instead delighted to have some occupants in the unit which was obviously her pride and joy. After lunch, he insisted that Camira rest, and she slept again like a child until the shadows were lengthening.

When she came through to the lounge finally, still looking warm and flushed from her sleep, it was to find him on the floor surrounded by a sea of newspapers, studying the racing form.

She said guiltily, 'It's so late! And nothing's ready for dinner.'

He looked up at her amusedly, 'It so happens it is. I picked up our dinner when I went out to get the papers. I thought you wouldn't mind a cold tea tonight?'

'Oh no,' she said hastily. 'I don't mind at all. What . . . what did you get?'

'Let's see,' he lay back on his elbows, 'I got some pâté from a delicatessen my stepmother patronises, also some smoked salmon and some ham off the bone, some of their special recipe apple and celery salad, also some of their potato salad. What else? Fresh asparagus and a tin of Camembert, some mangoes, and I replenished the wine rack. But I've just thought of something!' He sat up and Camira closed her eyes swiftly at the sight of his body clad only in a pair of shorts.

'What?' she asked breathlessly.

'Well, I suppose the asparagus has got to be cooked. But I'm blowed if I know how!'

She laughed at that. But she said gravely, 'If I promise not to over-exert myself, I might just be able to manage that.'

'All right. Providing you keep your promise,' he said lazily, and added, 'Why did you close your eyes just then, Camira? As if you were in pain?'

'Did I?' she asked with studied carelessness, and avoided his probing hazel gaze. 'I don't know.'

She moved to step around him, but he shot out a hand and caught her wrist. 'You wouldn't lie to me, would you?' he said softly but with an intent look. 'If there's anything else wrong with you, you would tell me, wouldn't you, Camira?'

'Yes,' she said reassuringly, and couldn't resist touching her fingers lightly to his for one brief moment. 'There's nothing, honestly. And . . . I'm very grateful for all this. Also sorry to have put you to so much trouble.'

He released her wrist and said wryly, 'I can think of worse kinds of trouble to be put to. And less comfortable surroundings too. Don't worry about it.'

He turned back to his papers and she retreated to the kitchen, thankful but conscious of a need to exercise more care.

They had their meal out on the terrace, protected from the slight breeze which was inevitable at this height and so close to the ocean, by a canvas awning.

'It's hot and humid down there,' Marc said idly as they lingered over their wine and cheese.

'Mmm,' she agreed.

'Have a mango. Here, I'll peel it for you.'

She watched his long fingers slice a portion of the golden-fleshed mango off the pip and cut a grid into it so that when he pushed the skin side inwards, the flesh stood up in a series of little rectangles ready to eat in the least messy manner of dealing with juicy mangoes.

He offered it to her and she took it and sighed, 'I get the feeling I'll end up as fat as pig if I stay here too long.'

He laughed. 'I'll let you know—if the danger arises. Have you ever played backgammon, Camira?'

'No.'

'Like to learn? Dad's got a beautiful set.'

'All right. As soon as I've cleared up. No,' she said steadily as he moved his shoulders, 'believe me, I feel guilty enough about the last time I left this place in a mess.' She stopped short and bit her lip. Why ever had she mentioned that? She went on in a rush, 'It's just a matter of popping everything into the dishwasher, isn't it?'

'Yes,' he said slowly. He picked up a fork and traced a pattern on the tablecloth with it. 'O.K.' He shrugged and lifted his eyes to hers in a brief uncommunicative glance. 'I'll set up the board while you do it.'

And Camira was chilled by the suddenly flat tone he'd used.

She proved an apt pupil and they spent the next few hours playing the game, and then to the accompaniment of Billy Joel in the background on the magnificent hi-fi set, they shared a nightcap.

'Bed for you, my dear,' Marc said finally with a glance at his watch. 'It's all of nine-thirty.'

She didn't demur, for in truth she felt a wash of real tiredness flow over her. But she knew as she climbed into that vast bed again that it wasn't so much due to her exertions of the previous weeks as the cold desperate knowledge that she had lied to herself for too long now. Whatever it was she felt for Marc Riley, it was no passing fancy, no mere subtle, mechanical chemistry of her body but something that would never leave her, something that she knew, somehow, she would never feel for anyone else. And she fell asleep with tears on her cheeks and a haunting refrain in her head. I love you just the way you are. . . .

And when the nightmare gripped her in the depth of the night, she woke screaming with sweat pouring off her and the crackle of flames in her head and the rending, tearing sound of metal on impact with a tall forbidding mountain range shrouded in a blue haze.

'No,' she sobbed. 'Please, no!'

The room was suddenly flooded with light and she jerked upright, not knowing where she was, her eyes wide and distended and the sobs still racking her body.

'For God's sake, Camira!' Marc crossed swiftly to the bed. 'What is it?'

'Oh,' she sobbed, and fell back against the pillows with her hands to her face. 'Nothing. It's nothing,' she gasped.

He sat down on the bed and pulled her up. 'It can't be nothing,' he said grimly with his hands on her shoulders. He gave her a little shake. 'Tell me,' he ordered.

'It's just a nightmare,' she stammered, and drew a ragged breath, unable to control a deep shudder.

He stared down at her and a muscle moved in his jaw. He relaxed his grip on her shoulders slightly and then brought one hand up to brush the hair from her eyes gently. 'Something to do with your parents?' he asked intuitively.

She nodded and shuddered again, unable to speak.

He drew her into his arms then and laid her head on his shoulder. 'The very best cure for nightmares,' he said matter-of-factly, 'is to tell someone about them. Is it the plane crash?'

She moved her head on his shoulder. 'Yes,' she said faintly. 'I see it and smell it and hear it as . . . as if I were there,' she faltered, and he lowered his head to catch her words.

'Does it happen often, Camira?' he asked quietly.

'N—no,' she said unsteadily. 'Not any more.' She stirred in his arms. 'I'll be all right now.'

'Maybe,' he agreed. 'But not just yet, I think.' He reached out behind her and at the touch of a switch on a panel beside the bed, the overhead light went out and she trembled in his arms immediately.

'I thought so,' he said briefly. 'Can you move over a little? I'm coming in. Don't worry, I won't stay or do anything we'll both regret. Just look on it as an act of kindness or a feeling of sympathy anyone would have for a stray waif.'

They lay side by side in the cool darkness, not touching but gradually Camira's breathing regularised and the inferno that she had seen so vividly subsided from her mind's eye and with a little sigh she turned towards him and was about to tell him that it was over, but he moved and pulled a pillow up behind him so that her head was now level with his waist, and began to stroke her hair absently.

She closed her eyes and thought, just a few more moments of heaven, then I can tell him. . . .

'Go to sleep, Camira,' he said gently. 'You're quite safe.'

CHAPTER NINE

WHEN she joined Marc on the terrace for breakfast the next morning, having woken to find herself alone and only the indentation of his head on the pillow to remind her of what had happened, she flushed and hesitated momentarily before stepping out to join him.

But he merely said, 'Good morning,' as his eyes roved over her impersonally. 'It's going to be another scorcher. Take it easy if you intend to swim or do anything out here today. You wouldn't want to add sunstroke to your problems.'

Of which I have so many. Camira added the unspoken implication to herself beneath her breath and blinked away a sudden tear.

'I will take it easy.' She looked at him, suddenly aware that he wasn't wearing shorts today but the kind of clothes he usually wore to the stables—long, well-fitting but faded twill trousers, riding boots', and his check shirt was unbuttoned almost to the waist as the still morning air gave promise of an almost tangible heat to come.

'Are you going out?' she asked.

'Mmm,' he nodded as he sipped his coffee. 'Bob rang up this morning. C'est Si Bon got herself cast in her stall last night.'

C'est Si Bon, Camira knew, was a particularly excitable, temperamental three-year-old filly. She said worriedly, 'I knew she'd do that one day! She always lies down so close to the wall.'

'Well, perhaps she's learnt her lesson now. They managed to get her up and she looks all right, but it depends how long she was lying there struggling. She's nominated for Southport tomorrow. I thought it would be a good idea if I looked her over. Couple of other things have come up too.'

Camira took a deep breath. 'I'll come with you,' she said quietly. 'I feel so much better. It won't take me a minute to pack.'

Marc looked her up and down before he said meditatively but with just a hint of steel behind his words, 'No. Since we began this cure, we'll do it properly. Just rest, today. And tomorrow you can come to the races with me if you feel up to it and we'll go back to Camira from there.' He stood up. 'I don't know what time I'll be back, I hope in time for dinner. See you then.'

He left her looking helplessly after him.

It was a long day. When the voluble cleaning lady had departed Camira tried to read one of the novels she found in the bookcase, but she couldn't concentrate. She switched on the television, but the choice of programmes seemed to consist solely of children's programmes, ancient black and white movies or a serial that was quite meaningless unless you had kept up with the previous episodes.

She switched the set off restlessly. What could she do? She wandered over to the bookcase again and this time her eyes alighted on a cookery book. That's it, she thought suddenly. I'll cook a special dinner. She pulled the book out and spent a pleasurable hour glancing through the recipes, then thoroughly inspected the contents of the pantry and the fridge and set to work.

By six-thirty, when dusk was drawing in swiftly, it was

all ready and the table in the alcove set attractively. Camira had decided it was too breezy to eat outside tonight. She had a quick shower and wished she had something more attractive to wear than the shorts and shirts she'd packed with such an effort and so little thought.

She stopped suddenly with her clothes in her hand and laid her forehead against the cool glass of the bedroom mirror. What is it you have in mind, Camira? she asked herself. Cooking him that meal, worrying about your clothes. Aren't you being a little stupid? After the things you said is he ever likely to ask you to marry him again? Is that what you've got in mind?

'Yes,' she answered herself out loud. 'Yes.' She sighed desolately. 'But it's much too late, isn't it? Didn't he say that? Although even he probably didn't realise how soon you'd come around to realising it.'

She traced the bevelled outline of the glass with one finger and then looked at her reflection levelly in the mirror. 'How superior you were, Camira,' she marvelled. 'How insufferably conceited, how *blind*! In fact there's no difference between you and Lisa Mackenzie really, is there?' She smiled bitterly at herself. 'Or rather,' she amended, 'there won't be unless you do something about this intolerable situation—quickly. But what?' she demanded of her reflection with just a trace of her old fire.

She turned away from the mirror and flinched at the answer that immediately presented itself to her. Could I? she wondered. Could I turn my back on Camira Lodge and Marc? It would be like tearing out a part of myself . . . both ways.

But then, she thought as she started to dress, isn't that better than being on everybody's conscience? She set her teeth as she recalled his words – we all feel guilty about you one way or another. Of course it's better! one part of her cried out. And anyway, how long can you go on being treated oh, so kindly but nonetheless like a stray dog!

But Marc didn't say a dog, he said a stray waif, she reminded herself, several hours later as she sat and waited and knew miserably that her Steak Diane and baked Idaho potatoes were wilting slightly in the warming compartment of the stove.

I should have made something more durable. She glanced at her watch. It was nine o'clock now. She stood up and stretched in the dark room. Somehow she hadn't felt like putting the lamps on. Then she heard the click of the front door and whirled around.

'Camira!' she heard him call.

'I'm in the lounge. I. . . .' She blinked as the lamp on the bar near the doorway sprang to life.

'What the hell are you doing in the dark?' Marc asked roughly, and she drew in a swift breath at the sight of him, tall and dark and strong but looking tired and dusty, and it was all she could do to prevent herself from crossing swiftly to him to kiss away his weariness, to cradle his body with her own.

She said instead, 'Is everything all right?'

He flung himself down in a chair and closed his eyes. 'Everything is all right now. But with horses, God knows how long it will stay that way.'

Camira crossed to the bar and poured him a drink. 'Tell me,' she said quietly.

Marc roused himself to take the drink from her. 'C'est Si Bon is the least of our problems. She was so fit this morning, in fact, she threw Marty and he broke his arm as he came down on the running rail.' Camira winced. He went

on, 'Good Time Gal chose this of all days to break a
pedal bone. She'll be out for months—if she isn't gone for
good. What else? Ah yes. Mission Beach has recovered
sufficiently from whatever ailed him to manage to pull
away from Bob this afternoon as he was leading him and it
took us two hours to catch him. Not that I'd have bothered—
he'd have come home as soon as his guts started rumbling,
but he jumped the fence and paraded up and down the
road with a supreme indifference for his own welfare, not
to mention the stream of cars and boats going down for a
spot of Friday night fishing.' He swore fluently and took a
pull of his drink.

'I'm sorry,' she said sincerely. 'Doubly so, since I've
been sitting here twiddling my thumbs. Are you hungry?
I made some dinner, but I'm not sure,' she said self-
consciously, 'what it's like. It was ready some time ago.'

Marc turned his hazel eyes broodingly on her. 'How
very wifely,' he commented dryly. 'Is that a gentle repri-
mand for my being late?'

She flushed but said coolly, 'Not at all. Perhaps you've
already eaten?'

'No, my dear Camira, I have not,' he said sardonically,
'so you may bring on your burnt offerings. Did you have
fun today playing at being a housewife? Did you find it
has any more appeal than it did not so long ago?'

She said steadily, 'That's not quite fair. I didn't
particularly want to be left here today. I didn't want to
come here in the first place. And so far as being house-
wifely, I don't think I've ever been any different. Not
wifely only.'

'How right you are. *Not* wifely. But undeniably domesti-
cated? Is that the right word?' he taunted her. 'It's a
strange combination, but then you're a strange girl. Your

ex-fiancé came looking for you today, by the way. I told him you'd gone on holiday. He was quite expansive, bared his heart to me, in fact. He seems to think he made a considerable error three years ago.' His hard eyes searched her face. 'Seems to think because you haven't found yourself a mate, he's still in with a chance. I wonder if he's right? Anyhow,' he went on, 'he's going to pursue you once he gets his hands on you again. Is that it, Camira? Despite what you think of David Thorpe you can't forget his . . . lovemaking? You only had to say, you know.'

She stared down at her hands unseeingly and thought she'd die at the pain he was inflicting on her.

'Is that why you surrendered so briefly even when you knew you didn't love me?' Marc asked contemptuously. 'Is it? I gave you a chance to retreat, but you didn't take it. Did you close those beautiful, cool eyes and pretend to yourself that it was David Thorpe kissing you? *Did* you?' he insisted.

'No,' Camira said brokenly, and wiped away a tear.

'Then what was it?' he demanded cruelly between his teeth.

'It wasn't!' she cried. 'It was. . . .' She faltered suddenly at his implacable look.

'Go on,' he said curtly

Her shoulders sagged. 'Perhaps it was,' she whispered, too defeated to care what she said.

He was on his feet in a flash and he pulled her into his arms. 'Perhaps this will teach you never to do it again, Camira Johnston,' he grated, and lowered his head to capture her lips in a brutal, savage kiss that seemed to last a lifetime. Camira made one attempt to break free, but that only brought her further punishment, and when he had finally done with her, she collapsed into the chair, unbelievably shaken, and raised a trembling hand to her bruised, swollen lips.

Marc loomed over her with both hands resting on either side of her on the arms of the chair and said softly but with a world of menace, '*Perhaps* you might find that embrace difficult to forget, too, my dear.'

She shrank back into the chair, her eyes alive with fear, but he straightened suddenly and said almost carelessly, 'Don't worry, Camira. You're quite safe with me now. You always will be.' He shrugged. 'And thank you, no, but I won't partake of your little dinner. I don't think I feel hungry anymore.' He moved to the bar and poured himself another drink, then threw himself down on the settee. 'Why don't you go to bed?' he said politely but with that old mockery in his voice. He glanced at her from beneath half-closed lids. 'Go to bed and dream of him. It might help cope with the nightmares,' he said wearily, and laid his head against the back of the settee and closed his eyes.

Camira stood up shakily and hestitated, but he didn't stir, didn't open his eyes, and she left the room quietly but with the sure knowledge that her heart was finally broken and, worse, it was all her own fault.

The peculiar thing about broken hearts, though, she discovered the next morning, was that they are in no way tangible, and however convinced of it you might be, you have nothing to show for it.

In other words, she told herself, it's just a meaningless phrase and no reason not to go on as you always have done. Especially if you're Camira Johnston, an unkind inner voice taunted.

'Well, and why not?' she murmured to herself as she

dressed. 'It's certainly going to help no one if you get around like a wet weekend. So you love him and you know you always will? It's still no guarantee that he loves you—far from it now, even if perhaps the tiniest seeds of it were ever there. And whichever way you'd gone about it who's to say it wouldn't have ended the same way? What you need is a bit of humour to see you through now until you've cut all the ties.'

This was so unfunny that she actually found herself smiling bleakly as she took a deep breath and squared her shoulders and forced herself to leave the seclusion of her bedroom.

Marc climbed out of the pool as she stepped on to the terrace where breakfast was laid out, and she felt an intense relief to realise that Mrs Thompson, the cleaning lady, must have already arrived.

She glanced at him briefly as he towelled himself vigorously and absolutely refused to allow her mind to dwell on the images his strong, hard body clad in brief blue bathing trunks could evoke so easily.

She said quietly, 'Good day,' as she unrolled her napkin. 'What time do we leave for the races?'

He sat down and regarded her quizzically for a moment, but the same resolution for once managed to quell the tell-tale colour that usually plagued her.

Finally he said, 'Eleven, thereabouts. Did you bring anything to wear?'

She raised her eyes from her bowl of fruit, caught off guard for a moment. 'Wear? What do you mean?'

He said evenly, 'Clothes. What else?'

'Well, yes. Jeans and a shirt . . . what's wrong with that?'

'I don't think they'd be too suitable for the members' enclosure,' he said flatly.

'True,' she said calmly. 'But they're eminently suitable for the stables and the saddling paddock. Which is where I'll be,' she added after a moment.

'I hesitate to contradict you, my dear Camira, but with Good Time Gal now scratched from this meeting, we'll only have one runner. And Bob and Tim can manage her. Besides, you'll be making up a foursome this afternoon. I've already accepted on your behalf.' Marc pushed his plate away lazily.

'Oh yes?' she said with ominous quiet.

'Yes,' he agreed. 'You and I and Lisa and David.' He laughed gently. 'Or perhaps I should rephrase—you and David and Lisa and I.'

She shot up out of her chair. 'No!' she spat at him furiously. 'Do you hear me? No! I. . . .'

'I hear you, Camira,' he said coldly. 'And so does everyone else, no doubt. Sit down. Or I'll make you,' he threatened.

She sank back into her chair, not for one moment doubting that he would do as he threatened, but while she had certain reservations about being manhandled, in a burst of clear, glorious anger from which humour was notably absent, she had no reservations about telling him what she thought of him—at that precise moment anyway.

'I hate you,' she said in a fierce undertone. 'And you have no right whatsoever to accept invitations on my behalf or to meddle in my affairs. 'I . . . I hate you!' she said again.

'Good,' he retorted, apparently unmoved. 'At least you're not feeling sorry for yourself any more.'

'I . . . I . . . how dare you!' she snapped passionately. 'Ju-just who do you think you are?' she spluttered.

'I dare,' he said, 'because I happen to know who I am. When you make someone party to your unfortunate affairs, when you swoon away in a dead faint at their feet, when you have ghastly nightmares in their presence,' his eyes narrowed slightly, 'not to mention something else you did, something . . . unforgivable, when you do all these things you should choose someone who can walk away from it all. But you've made yourself a flaming nuisance to me, Camira, and that's why I dare. That's why I'm presenting you to David Thorpe on a platter, and I hope to God he has the sense this time to sweep you off your feet and, if nothing else, get you out of my hair and off my property. Because I know that even if I could walk away from you—which under any other circumstances I could, my dear—to have you right next door like some lame dog, playing on Bob and Tim and everyone else's sympathy . . . well, it's just not on. So you'll come today,' he said softly, his eyes on her furious face and heaving breast and clenched fist, 'and if you try and hit me or throw anything at me, I'll put you over my knee and spank the living daylights out of you.'

Camira choked on her rage and Mrs Thompson, who had been hovering delightedly but unseen, rushed out and thumped her on the back and offered her a glass of orange juice, at the same time casting Marc a reproachful glance.

But if anything, he looked amused. He said lazily to her, 'Do you think there are any of my stepmother's clothes that would fit Camira, Mrs Thompson? I really can't take her to a champagne lunch at the races in jeans and a shirt, can I?'

Mrs Thompson pursed her lips. 'There's plenty there,' she offered. 'I know because I air them every now and then.' She glanced cautiously at Camira. 'Beautiful clothes, they are, and I'd say . . .' she nodded, 'yes, I'd say you'd be much of a size. Shall we try some?'

Marc answered her. 'Yeah,' he drawled. 'Take her away, will you, Mrs Thompson. But watch it,' he added softly on a note of suppressed laughter, 'she bites too.'

'Men!' Mrs Thompson sniffed a few minutes later when she had closed the door of the master bedroom and guided Camira, who was in danger of fainting from sheer frustrated rage, to a chair. 'I tell you, love, you need your wits about you when you tangle with 'em. Sit down here now,' she patted the velvet-covered chair. 'Tell you what, I'll just nip out and bring you a cup of coffee. It's still hot and you look as if you need it.' And she darted through the door and closed it firmly behind her.

Camira swallowed several times and promptly burst into tears. Mrs Thompson was back in no time with the coffee and she patted Camira's shoulders and murmured, 'There, there. Dry your eyes now, love.'

'But I can't wear his mother's clothes!' Camira hiccuped. 'I can't!'

'Don't see why not. She wouldn't mind. She's a dear, sweet, kind lady. . . .'

'That's not the point,' Camira said distraughtly.

But Mrs Thompson went on unheedingly, 'And anyway, love,' she said consolingly, 'the prettier you make yourself for him, the sooner this little tiff will be over. You mark my words.'

Being at that moment just so minded, Camira said, 'Want to bet?'

But Mrs Thompson was obviously an eternal romantic. 'Of course it will be. The more they care, the angrier they get sometimes. Now,' she advanced to a whole wall of built-in wardrobes and swept open a set of double doors, 'come over here and take a peep,' she said invitingly. 'Come on,' she added cajolingly.

Camira bit her lip. '*All right*,' she said suddenly, and added beneath her breath, if that's what he wants, that's what he's going to get. In a way it's the perfect solution. Perfect, Camira? she mocked herself. It's just the only solution.

Half an hour later when the bed was strewn with dresses and all sorts of outfits Camira said, 'What do you think of this one, Mrs Thompson?' She hadn't bothered to look at herself in the mirror, but the dress felt all right. It was a silky-knit halter-neck style that managed to look sophisticated but very cool. It was also, she thought as she looked down at herself to see the cleavage between her breasts exposed as was, she knew, most of her back and shoulders, a flaunting type of dress, and she wondered what category Marc's stepmother fell into. Someone who wore this kind of dress for her husband's eyes only?

'Ooh . . . yes,' Mrs Thompson enthused. 'Hang on,' she added sharply. 'No.' She clicked her tongue as she moved round behind Camira. 'No, dear, that won't do at all. Dear me!' And she giggled girlishly.

'What is it?'

'Bruises,' Mrs Thompson said succinctly. 'Here,' she drew Camira to the mirror. 'See? Round the tops of your arms and on your shoulderblades. See 'em?'

Camira peered awkwardly at herself in the mirror. She then shut her eyes and ground her teeth.

'There, there,' Mrs Thomspon soothed. 'They can be brutes, can't they? Still, wouldn't mind if my old man gave me a bruise or two occasionally. I sometimes think if I streaked down Cavill Avenue past the pub at five o'clock on a Friday afternoon and got meself on the front page of the Sunday papers, he'd still turn straight to the race results.'

Camira sank down onto the bed and dissolved into helpless laughter. 'Oh, Mrs Thompson,' she said as she wiped her eyes, 'you're marvellous, really you are. I don't know what you must think of me.'

'Listen, Miss Johnston, don't you worry your pretty head about it. I like who I like, whatever. And I like you. But I can tell there's someone who might get even crankier if we muck around for too long. I reckon *this* one.'

She pulled an outfit from the heap on the bed. It was a pencil-slim linen skirt with a slit up the front in an ivory beige, and to go with it there was a matching ivory silk short-sleeved jacket that crossed over at the front and fitted snugly over her hips to be tied at the waist with a quilted silk tie.

'Yes,' Mrs Thompson said determinedly, 'It's perfect. What about shoes now? Try these.'

'Oh . . . really. . . .' Camira protested, but subsided as she heard the shower being turned on in the adjoining bathroom.

'Y-e-s,' Mrs Thompson said happily as she knelt down and buckled the high ankle-strapped sandals to Camira's feet. 'Just adds a tough of colour,' she commented of the emerald green suede. 'How lucky your feet are the same size!'

'Very,' Camira agreed dryly. 'You'd be surprised if you knew how many people's shoes I can fit into.'

'Is that a fact, love?' Mrs Thompson stood up and surveyed the overall effect keenly. 'Hmmm. Just needs . . . let me think.' Her glance strayed down to her own ample bosom. 'That's it!' she cried excitedly, and wrenched the string of beads she wore off and clasped them around Camira's neck. 'Perfect,' she enthused. 'They match the shoes. My son brought them back from Fiji, they're rather unusual, aren't they? Don't look like they came from Woollies anyway,' she said with a chuckle, and added, 'which is more than you can say about the rest of me. Now, off you go and have a shower—you'll just be ready in time!'

Ready was the operative word, Camira discovered as she sat beside Marc in his powerful car. She doubted if she would ever be ready for the forthcoming encounter. She didn't have to glance sideways to bring his image to mind. In the closed confines of the air-conditioned car she was achingly aware of his virile masculinity that was heightened somehow by the fact that his thick dark hair was smooth and tidy now, his navy silk shirt and lightweight cream suit perfectly tailored and his shoes gleaming with the glow that only expensive leather achieves. If only he'd said one *kind* word, she thought longingly, I wouldn't go through with this plan.

But all he'd said since she'd emerged from the bedroom had been a brief, 'You'll do,' as his hazel gaze had raked her mercilessly from head to foot, and then he'd drawled, 'Still playing the virgin, I see. That should set him drooling.' And he'd picked up her bag and ushered her out of the unit ahead of him as if she'd been a paying guest.

She swallowed now and stared rigidly out of the window as they crossed the Nerang River Bridge to come into Southport. The City of the Gold Coast stretches from Southport at its northern end to Coolangatta on the New South Wales border and is a long golden beach broken occasionally by green-wooded headlands jutting into the sparkling sea. It is proudly Australia's premier holiday resort and apart from the fabulous beach it offers a diverse range of holiday accommodation and entertainment of every conceivable nature, Surfer's Paradise being the epitome of sophistication in the area. Added to this, the whole area had become a very desirable and sought after residential area with many magnificent luxury homes on canal developments.

But Camira was blind to this as she stared out of the window. The racecourse itself is situated in Southport and boasts every modern facility, but again she was oblivious to this as they swept to a halt in the members' car park. In fact all she could think of was the hard knot she could feel forming at the base of her stomach as she clenched her hands in her lap.

Marc switched the engine off and turned to her for the first time, one hand poised on the door-handle.

'Ready?' he said curtly.

She forced herself to dip her head in acknowledgement.

'Then for God's sake don't look so tortured about it,' he said roughly. 'We're not attending a wake.'

Oh, but we are, she thought sadly. And then for a moment she felt an unreasoning anger towards him, an anger that enabled her to say smoothly, lightly, 'I feel a bit like second-hand Rose! Does your stepmother come to the races often, I wonder?' she added with a little grimace.

'I wouldn't worry about that, my dear Camira,' he said smoothly. 'I doubt if Thorpe will be able to keep his eyes off you and I doubt if he'll notice your clothes at all. And don't try and tell me you're not aware of that.'

She shrugged and slipped out of the car. Marc got out too and for a moment their eyes clashed across the roof and Camira marvelled at how it was possible to love and to hate one man so intensely.

He was the first to turn away.

CHAPTER TEN

CAMIRA sat in the grandstand and watched C'Est Si Bon romp away with the first Novice of the day and surprised herself by cheering with the crowd, although not as exuberantly as Lisa Mackenzie.

Lisa was in an eye-catching garment that wavered between being a harem suit and a boiler suit in a clear, pure scarlet that complemented her magnificent tawny hair and olive skin. In fact she and Marc made a superbly eye-catching couple as Lisa threw her arms around him delightedly.

And she was at his side again in the winners' enclosure, posing prettily for the photographers with the horse's lead in her hand.

Camira wrenched her eyes away as Marc bent his head towards Lisa and said something to her that made her smile up into his eyes.

David was sitting beside her in the stand, seemingly at ease in the fashionable throng, but Camira knew he was bewildered and ever so slightly wary of her unexpected about-face. Lisa had been wary too as the champagne luncheon progressed when it had become clear that David Thorpe was very definitely Camira's escort; she had brightened and although it was simply not in her nature to allow any other female to blossom too freely in her company, she hadn't been outwardly hostile.

But despite Lisa's acceptance of her, Camira had found out that for her, the whole day had a totally unreal quality about it as if she were acting a part in a glamorous play, and she found herself wishing desperately, more than once, that she could do a Cinderella act and transform herself to a stablehand and remove herself to the infinitely preferable company of Tim and Bob.

David stirred beside her and said, 'If I'm any judge this means more champagne. Shall we rejoin our host?'

'David. . . .' Camira stopped and took a deep breath. It had to be done, she thought wildly. And anyway there had to be some compensations, surely. Horses. . . .

'David,' she said again, 'do you still want to marry me?'

David went quite still beside her. He wasn't looking at her, but out across the track and it was a long moment before he turned his blue eyes to her and she saw the incredulous look in them and a tinge of—was it joy?

'Camira,' he said finally and then unsteadily, 'no . . . I was going to ask a whole lot of questions, but just one will do. And it's simply this. When?'

'Whenever you like. As soon as possible. But,' she coloured faintly, 'I . . . until . . . what I mean is. . . .'

'You mean you're not prepared to sleep with me until the knot is tied? Is that it, Camira?' He took one of her hands in his. 'You didn't have to tell me that. I've learnt something over the last years. God! I think I need something stronger than champagne. Let's get out of here!'

'There's just one other thing, David.'

'Name it, pet,' he said promptly.

'I'd rather we kept it to ourselves for a while. I . . . I'm going home to Camira tonight and I'll have to tie up a few loose ends. I thought I'd put my place on the market and I . . . well. . . .' she shrugged rather helplessly.

He stared at her with faintly narrowed eyes, 'I get you,' he said finally. 'All those kind people up there, including Jane Sinclair to name but one, will delight in trying to talk you out of it. Is that it?'

'Yes,' she said gratefully, and thought with a wry inward grimace, even if that's not the reason, it'll be a problem!

'All right,' he said seriously. 'We'll tell no one if you promise me one thing, Cam. We'll name today fortnight as our wedding day?'

She nodded, but her silly heart took a sickening lurch.

He said lightly, 'May I come and see you once or twice between now and then? Just to assure myself it's no dream?'

'Of course.'

David played his part perfectly for the rest of the afternoon, solicitous of Camira, but no more so than he'd been earlier, and if there was a slight flush to his features which brought an oddly thoughtful look to Marc Riley's face occasionally, it could have been explained by the fact that he was drinking quite heavily. At least Camira devoutly hoped that was what Marc would think.

It was Lisa who suggested after the last race that they all go out together that evening and celebrate. 'Let's have dinner and dance the night away, darling. Part of the night anyway,' she murmured coaxingly as she stroked Marc's coat-sleeve.

Marc looked down at her upturned face and grinned. Camira held her breath because she knew she could stand just so much but no more.

But he said lightly, 'Not tonight, my sweet. I think we've celebrated pretty thoroughly as it is. Besides, Camira's only just off the convalescent list. We wouldn't want her to overdo it.' He sent a mocking glance in Camira's direction.

Lisa pouted. 'David can take her home, can't he? Besides,' she struck an attitude as if something had just dawned on her, 'I don't quite understand Camira's position.' She was unable to keep a slight note of aggression out of her voice like a spoilt child wanting to strike out at the person she saw as interfering with her pleasures. 'What is it exactly you do, darling?' she asked, turning her tawny eyes on Camira, her voice rising slightly. 'You're certainly a very privileged employee.'

Camira was conscious of several things. That the crowded elegant bar they were drinking in had gone fractionally quieter. That David had tensed and sat forward as if to speak. That Marc Riley's eyes were resting on her but were quite enigmatic.

She said evenly. 'I don't know about privileged, Lisa, but I won't be an employee for much longer. And really if you and Marc would like to go out, don't worry about me. David will take me home.'

She registered the fact that David relaxed, as did Lisa herself, but her employer for some inconceivable reason of his own refused to accept the out she had offered.

He said casually, 'I wasn't only thinking of Camira, as it happens. We got problems back at the ranch, as they say. I do want to get home now. No point in you going out of your way, David. Perhaps you'd see Lisa home for me? Good,' he said as David shrugged rather bewilderedly. He stood up, and even Lisa followed suit at the decisive note in his voice.

They made their farewells in the car park, Lisa effusively but with just a hint of tears held at bay, and Marc was unexpectedly gentle with her.

David openly made arrangements to come out and see Camira in a few days' time, which she agreed to quietly, but as they drove away she couldn't help but see a look of puzzled speculation on his face, and she cursed Marc Riley fluently but silently as the car responded to the dictates of his lean, powerful hands and surged along the Pacific Highway towards home.

It was a silent journey and he drove at a frightening speed until Camira said disjointedly, 'The police . . . they . . . sometimes set up a radar trap. . . .'

He laughed harshly. 'Let 'em try and catch me! What did you mean back there?'

'I've made some plans, that's all.'

'I take it you don't intend to enlighten me,' he drawled.

'Not yet,' she said steadily. 'Not until they're more than just i-ideas.' She stumbled slightly over the last word.

He glanced at her briefly. 'Thorpe any part of them?' he queried.

'Perhaps,' she said stiffly, and he laughed again.

'Perhaps my foot,' Marc said inelegantly. 'He was getting himself quite drunk on your mere presence, cool as it was, my dear Camira. He'll fall in with any plans you care to make, my instincts tell me,' he added cynically. 'All you have to do is name the day—but I gather you're going to play coy for a while.'

She opened her mouth, but shut it almost immediately and turned her head to gaze unseeingly out of the window. Marc said no more, and it wasn't until she was home in her own little cottage and his car was edging down the uneven driveway that she allowed herself to wonder why it was that she couldn't bring herself to tell him.

She was pleased and gratified the next morning to find her

garden in tip-top condition, and she felt an incredibly warm rush of affection for Tim and Bob who had contrived this despite all their other problems.

Then, in the early morning sunlight, all her delight turned to ashes at the thought of how soon she would be parting with it all, and for the first Sunday for many months she didn't have the heart to open her wayside stall. Instead, mindful of how shorthanded without Marty they would be at the Lodge and despite a curious reluctance, she climbed the fence and walked to work.

There was no doubt Tim and Bob were delighted to see her on her own account, nor did they protest overmuch when she laughingly turned aside their suggestions that she might not yet be quite fit to work.

'It's great to have you back, lass,' said Bob later in the morning as they worked side by side. 'The old place didn't seem the same without you. But didn't I tell you the boss would look after you if you did the right thing by him?' He beamed at her with simple pride.

Tim was even more enthusiastic if anything. 'You look great, Camira,' he said with boyish admiration. He sobered suddenly. 'I could kick myself for . . . for not realising how you were overdoing things. At least,' he amended, 'I could see, but I didn't know how. . . . Anyway,' he smiled suddenly, 'Marc found the right solution, didn't he? I told you there's a heart of gold somewhere there, didn't I?'

'You did indeed, Tim,' she said with an effort. 'How's Julie? And Cooper's Creek?'

'Ah,' said Tim in an unconscious echo of his brother. 'Julie is trotting very creditably and Coop is just marvellous.'

Camira burst out laughing. 'You make it sound as if Julie's a horse and Coop a girl, Tim!'

'Did I?' he asked with comical anxiety. 'I didn't mean to!'

She worked on steadily through the long hot morning. She hadn't been so foolish as to imagine she would be able to avoid her employer, but what she hadn't bargained for was his easy-going manner, as if nothing momentous had ever occurred between them. There was the same camaraderie with herself just ever so slightly on the outer— from his point of view anyway. And if it cost him the slightest effort to maintain this front, there was no evidence of it, and she was forced to conclude that it was no mask but that he had decided to put the whole thing behind him and found it particularly easy to do so. And if her heart hadn't already felt like some frozen alien object in her breast, it did so now, but it hardened slightly if anything.

The next morning she rang a real-estate agent and put her property on the market. The only stipulation she made was that she didn't want any For Sale signs on the place until she left. She spent the next few days pottering quietly amongst her plants, riding with Tim and Julie and each day doing her four-hour stint at the stables. Jane and Alan were still away and it was David who provided her only company at home that week other than Tim and Julie, who popped in whenever they were hungry. Which was often. Tim seemed determined not to allow a recurrence of the previous week's events and he chided her constantly about doing too much.

David arrived on Wednesday afternoon, and he brought with him a surprising idea.

He said as he balanced a cup of tea on his knee and looked around the lounge,

'You know, Cam, you've worked miracles with this corner of the old place. And the cottage. I've never been inside it before.'

'Haven't you?' she murmured as she sat down herself. She was hard put to it to say exactly how she felt confronted now as she was with David in the flesh. During the preceeding days he had become somewhat shadowy and unreal in her mind, and indeed she had often stopped and asked herself if she had really asked David—David Thorpe of all people—to marry her, or if it was not some figment of her imagination.

But the illusion was now firmly dispelled. He was no doubt there, sitting opposite her with his own familiar brand of confidence as unchanged as was his fair hair and his blue eyes, and she shivered suddenly.

'What is it? Someone walk over your grave?' he queried lightly but with that faint air of speculation in his eyes again.

Camira tried to smile, and he frowned fleetingly and put his teacup aside.

'Cam,' he said seriously, 'there's obviously something going on that I don't understand. No,' he held up his hand as she tried to speak, 'I'm not going to ask for any explanations. Believe me, where you're concerned I'm just counting my blessings—whatever. But I did wonder if one of your problems anyway, could be the thought of leaving Camira.' He sat forward and said urgently, 'But we don't have to leave. You've got plenty of space down here, in the house as well as outside. We could build some stables for my team, fence off some yards. What do you say?' he asked eagerly.

'No! No,' she repeated less forcefully.

'But why not?'

'Because. . . .' She stood up and walked to the screen door with her arms folded around her as if she was in pain. 'Because I should have made a move years ago.' She turned to face him. 'It's no good staying on here, David. I really want to leave.'

'All right,' he said finally. 'Whatever you say. I guess it's natural to feel you should put it all behind you.' His eyes searched her face and he added with a wry grin, 'You haven't even asked me where I live now. On Saturday week, for all you know, you could be stepping off a precipice. Doesn't that bother you, Cam? I should feel flattered, but somehow I don't.'

She moistened her lips. 'David, if you want to pull out you only have to say so. I realise I was rather presumptuous at the races.'

He put his head on one side and said consideringly, 'As a matter of fact you weren't. Only, shall we say, unexpected, and you caught me a trifle off guard. But as I've said before, I'm not quibbling. And I've put everything in hand, Cam. We're to be married at noon, not this Saturday but the next. Will you be ready then?'

'Yes,' she said. 'Yes.'

He stood up and touched her cheek with a finger. 'I wonder.'

'I will,' she avowed shakily.

David said, 'I won't see you before then, Camira, but if you want to talk to me one phone call will summon me like a genie. Goodbye—for now, my love,' he said quietly.

'Goodbye for now, David,' she said steadily, but conscious of threatening tears, and for a long time after the last sounds of his car had faded, she sat in her darkening living room with her anguished thoughts.

She knew she could never love him, knew that her love was reserved for ever for one man. And yet somehow she felt as if she was doing David an injustice. He's changed, she thought. Or—what was it Marc had once said? When a

man has lust in his heart. . . . Perhaps what she'd thought
of as a shallow, conceited, shabby feeling had been deeper
than she had realised. Too late, Camira, she told herself.
You've worked it all out too late. Whatever he did to you
once, he's not quite the same man now. And the knowledge
that she was using David brought a feeling of hollowness.
Could it help in this marriage? she pondered. But in her
heart of hearts she knew nothing would make it easier to
marry another man, and she closed her mind to anything
beyond Saturday week.

The Sinclairs arrived home the following day, brimming
and bubbling with vitality—at least Jane and the twins
were, but Alan confided in Camira, in an uncharacteristic
burst of eloquence, that he was exhausted and coming
home would be like a rest.

'Talk,' he said grimly. 'If you think Jane's bad wait
until you meet her mother and father!'

'I have,' said Camira. 'They used to live around here
too, remember?'

'Oh, they're not so bad!' Jane countered, and then giggled. 'Well, maybe. Anyway, seeing that you're so dead set
against a bit of chat, why don't you take the twins home now
that Camira's resumed their acquaintance and leave me
here to have a good long heart-to-heart with her? Everything's unpacked and they're ready for their nap now too.'

'Will do,' Alan said briefly, and scooped up his offspring
in a large arm. 'See you, Camira.'

'See you, Alan,' Camira replied with a grin. She turned
to Jane as they disappeared down the driveway. 'What
have you been doing to him? He looks positively thin!
You cruel, heartless wife.'

Jane sighed and then giggled again. 'I don't think he'll
ever really hit it off with my mother, and besides, he's

never really happy when he's away from home for too long. He'll be right in no time. Now, tell me all the news, love. I gather,' she added slyly, 'that you took off for the big smoke for a few days. In the company of your devastating employer. Having worked yourself into the ground!' Her tone changed to one of reproach. 'Really, I can't let you out of my sight for a minute, Camira!'

Camira sighed and shrugged. 'Is nothing ever secret around these parts?' she said plaintively. 'Who've you been talking to?'

'Mrs Gregory. I went in to get some milk. Came out with the most curious news I've heard in a while,' Jane said humourously. 'So tell your Aunt Jane, my pet, before she dies of curiosity.'

Camira told her. Most of it anyway. In fact you could say a severely edited version, she told herself with a slight smile. The problem is, she reminded herself, Jane has this uncanny knack of seeing through my editing.

But Jane seemed to be too round-eyed to be poking any holes in Camira's story and she demanded a step-by-step description of the unit in Surfer's and all the luxuries it contained.

'Wow!' she breathed finally. 'Sounds like some pad! Did you swim in the pool? It's almost worthwhile having a nervous breakdown once in a while, if that's the kind of treatment it can bring, I tell you!'

'I did not have a nervous breakdown, Jane!'

'Well, whatever it was,' Jane said airily, 'you must have been pretty crook for him to stay with you. Er . . . . I take it you two get on better now? You don't still dislike him, do you.'

'No,' Camira said hastily, 'of course not. Jane?' But she stopped there. How could she tell her about David?

'What is it, love?'

'Nothing. Just glad to see you all back.' Coward, she taunted herself. You have to tell her some time, and soon.

But by midway through the following week she had still told no one, and it was with an increasing feeling of desperation that she set about that evening to sort through her things with some intention of packing.

It was Tim who disturbed her in this task. He drove up and stopped with a beep of the horn beneath her windows to announce his arrival. He had recently been given the freedom of one of the Lodge vehicles since his sixteenth birthday and for a time this had even erased the pleasure of using Coop as a mode of transport.

'You there, Camira?' he called as he bounded into the house. 'Gosh!' he stopped short and eyed the mess. 'Whatever are you doing?'

'Spring-cleaning, Tim,' she replied with a quiver of guilt as she emerged from a kitchen cupboard. 'But I'm always willing to stop for you. Like some homemade lemonade?'

'Under any other circumstances I'd love some, but I'm a man with a mission tonight, believe it or not,' he said happily. 'Marc wants to see you and I've been entrusted with the job of transporting you safely to Camira Lodge. How about that?'

'You must have improved, Tim,' she said with a grin. 'It's all of a mile by road.' She sobered. 'What does he want?'

'Didn't say,' Tim answered laconically, 'but then again he didn't sound as if it would be a good idea to put him off. You know—firm and resolved.' He deliberately deepened his voice. 'Go and fetch Camira for me, would you, Tim, and if you put a scratch on her or the ute, watch it, mate.'

'Oh, Tim,' Camira laughed, 'you're very funny, did you know? Well, I suppose I have no choice. Just let me wash my hands.'

But she wasn't quite so amused as she climbed the front steps to the house. It had been unfair to send Tim for her and she felt a tremor of apprehension. What on earth could he want her for that he couldn't say to her the following morning?

She was still eyeing Marc warily as he ushered her into the study and thanked her for coming. 'Would you like a drink, Camira?' He turned to Tim. 'That will be all, thanks, old son. You can put your mechanical steed to bed, I'll take her home.'

'Right-ho!' said Tim with a tinge of disappointment, but he left the room and closed the door.

'Drink?' Marc said to Camira again.

'No. Yes, thank you, I will. Whatever you're having.'

'Scotch,' he said briefly, and poured two. She accepted hers with a murmur of thanks and watched him sit down behind the desk. He wore dark blue jeans and a blue and white striped shirt with the sleeves casually rolled up to the elbows and the front unbuttoned almost to the waist.

He didn't speak immediately but stared down at the glass in his hand with an almost brooding expression.

'You . . . wanted to see me,' Camira said at last, her nerves stretched.

'Uh-huh.' He swirled the liquid in the glass and then raised his dark eyes to hers swiftly. 'Tell me, Camira, are you any further forward with your plans?'

'Yes.'

'Care to elucidate?'

'No,' she replied stonily.

'Well then, perhaps I might. Where are you going to

go when you find a buyer for your property? Bearing in mind that you're speaking to a prospective purchaser.'

'What?' she gasped, and jerked upright in her chair. 'What do you mean? How . . .?'

'How did I know?' he said smoothly. 'One of life's little coincidences, you might say. The real-estate agent you approached is a bright young man and he did a bit of research and discovered that it was originally attached to this property. He then approached me with the sound business proposition that even if I might not have a use for the acreage now, in the long term when this area's opened up, as it no doubt will be, bearing in mind that Surfer's Paradise was once a mangrove swamp too, I couldn't lose on it.'

'Oh,' was all she could find to say.

'Precisely,' Marc said ironically. 'Which led me to wonder, in view of the fact that he also told me that I could have vacant possession at the end of this week, just where you intended going. And for that matter whether you intended to give me any notice at all or whether you were going to walk out and leave us high and dry at the stables, my dear Camira.'

A hand flew to her mouth and she flinched visibly, not only at his sardonic tone but at this dreadful oversight on her part. In the mental turmoil of the previous week she had completely overlooked this one factor.

'I'm sorry,' she stammered, and blushed fierily, 'I can't think why . . . I should have mentioned it! I'm sorry,' she added lamely. 'Are you . . . really going to buy it?' she stammered.

'Possibly,' he said expressionlessly. 'No doubt the thought fills you with horror. Or perhaps not.'

'What do you mean?' she asked after a moment.

'I merely wondered if the course of true love was going so smoothly for you that you could now view the rest of the world, including me, through rose-coloured glasses. If you were so bedazzled that's why you even forgot to give us any notice,' he added contemptuously.

Camira set her teeth at his tone. 'That's my affair,' she said evenly.

'Is it?' Marc got up and refilled his glass. 'You have a funny way of going about your affairs. I could understand you wanting to walk out on me without so much as a backward glance, but I find it a bit odd that you could do it to people who are genuinely fond of you like Tim and Bob. Not to mention your best friend Jane.'

Her eyes flew to his face. 'Have you . . . did you tell her?' she whispered.

'No.' He didn't resume his seat but stood leaning back against the wall. 'However, I did tell Alan inadvertently this evening. He was surprised, to say the least.'

'You mean,' she said furiously, 'that you deliberately went down there and told him!'

'Not at all. I took a horse down to stand him in the salt water. It's very good for their legs—but I'm sure you know that. Alan was fishing off the wharf and we chatted for a while. The conversation turned to yourself, quite naturally, and I merely expressed some curiosity about your movements when you leave here. I had no idea, you see, that you planned to run out on them too.'

'I did not plan to run out on them!' she muttered between her teeth.

'No?' he queried with idly raised eyebrows. 'Then you're leaving it a little late, aren't you?' he commented dryly. 'Or is it that it's unexpectedly hard to tell Jane Sinclair

that you're running away to live with Thorpe? To become
his mistress?'

Camira went suddenly still. 'Why do you assume—that?'
she asked through stiff lips.

'What else is there to assume? I'm sure,' he added with
narrowed eyes, 'that if it were any other way David would
have told the world by now. But even he might find he's
troubled by a pang of conscience or two to let it be known
that you've finally given in to him.'

'That's funny,' she said in a strangled voice. 'After all,
I do remember you giving me, or rather giving him, through
me, some very similar advice. Sweep me off my feet were
your exact words, if you recall.'

He raised his eyebrows ironically. 'I recall them. But I
must admit I didn't think you'd fall over like a ninepin
fitted with a self-destruction device. You held out for
three years to get him to marry you and now you've
blown it all. And what I wonder is—why? You don't
surely imagine you're getting some kind of a revenge on
me, do you, Camira? For some of the hometruths I told
you?'

'Oh!' she gasped, more furiously angry than she'd
ever been in her life. 'You . . . I don't understand you!'

'That's obvious,' he drawled.

But she swept on regardless. 'It's perfectly all right—in
your book—for me to sleep with *you* because I might
want to, your words again, but quite a different matter
when it's David. *Then* I become a self-destroying ninepin
and heaven knows what else besides! I really think you're
drawing a fine line of difference. In fact to me it's an
invisible line!'

Marc moved his shoulders against the wall and drawled,
'Your memory has some blank spots in it, obviously,

Camira. You seem to forget that I also wanted to marry you.'

'Marry me?' she spat at him. 'Let's just set the record straight for once and for all. You wanted to sleep with me. You uttered not one word of love or even affection—or of anything other than a basic lust.' She stopped and drew a sharp breath. There, it was out. An admission she hadn't even made to herself before. An admission she should never have made to him. She went on hurriedly, coldly, 'Not that it would have made any difference, but nevertheless, I'm not quite stupid, you know.'

'Aren't you?' he queried mockingly. 'Sometimes actions speak louder than words, my dear Camira, but you have to have everything spelt out in words of one syllable. . . .'

'Don't keep calling me that!' she cried distractedly.

'Of course, I forgot,' he said sardonically. 'Camira's out and *Cam's* the in thing now, isn't it? I wonder how your grandfather would like it?'

She placed her half empty glass down on the desk with a very deliberate movement and tensed as he laughed softly and said,

'You don't fool me for one moment, you know. You'd love to throw that glass at me, wouldn't you? But it might not be very wise.' He straightened up and tossed off the rest of his drink. 'Shall we go?' he said casually.

'I will go,' Camira said clearly, and stood up. 'I know my way around outside blindfolded and I don't need *you* to escort me anywhere.'

She stood her ground as he advanced towards her.

'But you're going to have me whether you like it or not,' he said softly but with a distinct gleam of menace in his hazel eyes. 'You have a choice. I can carry you out of here or you can walk beside me. What's it to be, my dear, sweet little Camira?' he added deliberately.

She swallowed, aware that his proximity was having the same old effect on her treacherous heart. 'Very well,' she said stiffly, 'I'll walk.'

'Very wise,' he commented. 'Could it be that you're learning some caution at last?'

She didn't reply but lowered her head and took a deep breath. He strolled to the door. 'After you, ma'am.'

They accomplished the short journey in total silence, but as Marc brought the car to a halt at her verandah, he said coolly, 'Good luck on your venture, Camira, whatever it is. And whatever other water has flowed under the bridge, I must say you're one of the best strappers I ever had.'

She stared at him uncertainly with her hand on the door. 'Are you . . .?'

'Yes,' he agreed, 'I'm saying goodbye. I have to go to Melbourne for a couple of days. I've made arrangements to replace you, but if you want to work out your last few days, I'm sure Bob would be only too pleased. And if I do decide to buy—this,' he waved a hand, 'no doubt it can be arranged through our respective solicitors. As a matter of fact if Bob and Mrs Leonard do tie the knot, which seems to be the latest update on that situation, it would be an ideal spot for them, don't you think?'

'I . . . yes,' she stammered, unable to tear her eyes from his as she digested this. 'Yes,' she said again, and licked her lips.

'Perhaps we should shake hands?' Marc said expressionlessly, and took her free hand into his. Camira let it lie there, unable to restrain a sudden tremor that moved up her arm that the contact with him brought on.

They stayed like that for what seemed like a small eternity, in the warm darkness. Then he released her hand after a brief gentle pressure on it and turned away. 'Goodbye, Camira,' he said evenly.

She closed her eyes to hide her tears. 'Goodbye . . . Marc,' she murmured, and slipped out of the car and into the cottage.

CHAPTER ELEVEN

'So you've been holding out on us, lass?' Bob said genially. 'Where are you going? And what will you be doing?'

It was the next morning, and as Bob spoke Camira couldn't help noticing that Tim, who was working in the next stall, stiffened and rested his pitchfork momentarily.

'I'm . . . getting married, Bob,' she said with an effort.

'Shucks!' Bob grinned ruefully. 'Must be the silly season,' he said with a shake. 'So'm I.'

'So I heard, Bob, I'm very happy for you both.'

'Thanks, love. Who're you marrying?' he asked conversationally.

Camira was aware that Tim had stopped working again. 'David Thorpe,' she said. 'Do you . . . I suppose you know him?'

''Deed I do,' said Bob after a moment of hesitation. 'Hey, Tim?' he called out. 'Hear the good news?'

Tim threw down his pitchfork and came slowly towards them. 'Yes, I heard. Congratulations, Camira,' he said, but without quite meeting her eyes. He turned quickly at the sound of horses' hooves against a wall. 'That's C'Est

Si Bon playing up. I'll go and sort her out.'

'Is he all right?' Camira said tentatively to Bob as Tim hurried away.

Bob shrugged. 'Why don't you go and ask him? He's very fond of you, you know.'

'I . . . will,' said Camira and put the bridle she had in her hands down on the floor. She didn't see Bob's anxious eyes following her.

'Tim?' Camira rounded a corner to find Tim sitting on a bale of lucerne looking both glum and dejected. 'What is it, Tim?' she asked gently. 'I'm sorry, I shouldn't have sprung this news on everyone the way I did.'

He looked up at her fleetingly and then down at his hands again. 'It's not that—so much anyway, Camira.'

'Well, what is it, Tim?'

'Nothing. It's nothing,' he sighed, and then said exasperatedly, 'It's just that I thought you two would be so perfect for each other. You and Marc. I'm so fond of him, I always have been,' he said helplessly. 'And you're the one girl who's so right for him in every way.'

'Tim,' she began shakily, and stopped to take a grip on herself. 'Tim, you've just paid me the most fabulous compliment,' she said gently. 'But it can't be . . . that way. It just can't.'

'I suppose not. Not if you love someone else. I suppose,' he said with a strained laugh, 'you think I'm just a silly kid. But when he and Lisa had that row over you. . . .' He stopped abruptly and then shrugged. 'I couldn't help overhearing,' he mumbled.

'When . . . when was this?'

He shrugged again. 'Ages ago. When she was staying here. That's why she left. Actually she didn't have any choice. He more or less threw her out. That's when I began to wonder, began to hope. . . . I didn't know how you felt for someone else, though.'

Camira said disjointedly, 'Even if it weren't that way, Tim, surely, you can see that we just don't get on that well. I mean, we've been arguing since the first moment we met, don't you remember?'

He smiled faintly. 'Yes. You know, my mother often says that Marc is a great deal like my . . . our father. Much more so than I am. And she says she feels sorry for the girl he finally falls for because when he does finally fall, he'll go like a ton of bricks. And neither of them will know what's hit them. She should know, I guess. They've been together—our parents—for seventeen years, and you'd sometimes think they'd only been married yesterday.'

'Your father was lucky to find your mother after losing his first wife.'

'He didn't lose her. She walked out on him and left him high and dry with a six-month-old baby. And for the next ten years apparently he had only one thought where women were concerned—take what you could from them. Love 'em and leave 'em, in other words. Until he met my mother. I think he's always regretted that and wondered if Marc didn't inherit some of that bitterness. But not, as yet, the cure for it. Camira, will you write to me? I know this is just a silly teenage boy's fancy, but I'll always think of you as a sister I'd have loved to have had.'

'Of course, Tim. Of course,' was all she could find to say.

But not—as yet—the cure.

Tim's words kept repeating themselves over and over in her mind as she climbed the fence and walked to the cottage. Only one sixteen-year-old boy's theory, she reminded herself just as often, and stopped dead as she walked into the living room of the cottage. Jane got up from one of the armchairs.

They stared at each other until finally Camira spoke.

'You know,' she said flatly, and moved to the sink to fill the kettle.

'You're wrong, Camira,' said Jane in a low voice. 'I don't know anything beyond the fact that you're leaving on Saturday. But I have this dreadful premonition. You're going away with David, aren't you?'

'Et tu, Brute,' Camira muttered to herself, and closed her eyes briefly. She turned to Jane. 'Look,' she said hardly, 'I'm going to *marry* David on Saturday. What's so inconceivable about that? I've already been engaged to him once before.'

'Camira!' Jane cried. 'It's me you're talking to. The same person who sat here only a few weeks ago and heard you admit you'd *never* loved him. Why are you doing this?'

'He's . . . he's changed, Jane.'

Jane said wearily, 'I wouldn't know.' She shrugged. 'He might have, but that's not the point. You haven't changed and don't try to pretend to me that you have! Instead, answer me honestly if you dare. Why are you doing this and in this manner?'

Camira let out a long sigh. 'Very well,' she said steadily, 'I'll tell you. I fell in love with Marc like . . . I didn't believe it was possible to fall in love with anyone. But so far as I could work out, women are nothing but a game to him, and,' she paused and twisted her fingers together, 'even something I heard very recently—well, I suppose it could be taken either way,' she said distractedly. 'All I know is that I'd rather die than become one of his cast-offs, and I can't, I just can't go on living right next door to him, virtually in his pocket. It's as simple as that,' she added baldly. She dropped her head into her hands and started to sob.

'Oh, Camira,' Jane sighed, and drew her into her arms. 'Love, why didn't you tell me? Isn't that what friends are for? And none of this explains why you're going to marry David.'

Camira raised her tear-streaked face. 'Because that's what Marc himself advised me to do,' she said fiercely, 'and that's what I'm going to do.'

Camira sat in a straight-backed chair so as not to crush her wedding outfit and stared at the telephone beside her as she fiddled with the small posy of carnations Jane had brought her earlier.

She had got ready far earlier than she had needed to and a small overnight bag stood in the middle of the room while a row of neatly stacked cardboard cartons packed with her possessions lined one wall. She had decided to sell the furniture with the property.

She removed her gaze from the telephone and looked down at the new outfit she'd purchased specially for her wedding. She hadn't had the heart to ask Jane to take her shopping, but she'd managed to cadge a lift into Beenleigh with Mrs Gregory and also managed to keep the purpose of her shopping trip secret. Not that she really cared one way or another what she was married in, but she felt she owed David something. So she'd emptied her savings bottles and besides the outfit she was now wearing had bought herself a matching set of silk underwear and a sheer fine white nightgown and robe.

The dress itself wasn't white but the palest lavender colour that was almost grey but not quite, and the material was fine and filmy over a delicate matching lining. The bodice of the dress was loose with a blouson effect and a series of small pin-tucks into the shoulder seams and a plain revere collar and short sleeves. It was gathered into the waist and the skirt was full and swirled around her as she walked and ended about two inches below her knees, which the saleslady had assured was the latest fashion. Her slender-heeled shoes were of grey kid, as was her small clutch bag, and the carnations were a creamy white.

She raised them to her face now and rested their cool damp petals against her cheek. She stayed thus for a long moment, staring unseeingly across the room. Then she stiffened as she heard a car drive up and stop below the verandah. She felt as if she was pinned to chair, unable to move a muscle as she heard footsteps on the verandah and then the familiar squeak as the screen door opened. She swung round, her heart beating fast, and gasped.

Because it was Marc Riley who stood in the doorway surveying her with a look of cold, mocking insolence.

'What . . . why are you here?' she stammered, taking in his elegant lightweight grey suit, pale blue shirt and navy silk tie. He looked superbly groomed but with a faint air of weariness that touched her heart unwittingly.

His words brought her to feet and immediately dispelled any tender feelings she was experiencing.

He said coolly with a glance at his watch, 'I've lined up a marriage celebrant who's expecting us in exactly fifty-five minutes. We don't have much time to chat.'

'You've *what*?' she gasped incredulously.

'You heard me, Camira,' he said roughly. He looked round and his eyes alighted on her overnight bag. He strode over to it and picked it up. 'Ready?' he asked briefly.

'I . . . No! I'm not marrying you! I'm . . . I. . . .'

'I know,' Marc said tautly. 'You were expecting to marry David Thorpe this morning. He'll survive being left virtually at the altar, believe me. He survived without you for three years. And I can tell you he wasn't too noticeably bereft.'

'Look,' she said shakily, and backed away from him as he dropped the bag to the floor and advanced towards her with the hard light of battle in his hazel eyes, 'can't we discuss this at least?' she pleaded huskily.

'As you once commented,' he said dryly, and took her chin in his fingers, 'I'm not a great one with words. But I'll say this, sweetheart,' she flinched at the mockery in his voice, 'unless you want me to rip that beautiful dress off your beautiful body and make violent love to you right here on the floor, you'll not only come quietly but you'll stay quiet until the thing is done. And then you can talk as much as you like. Do I make myself perfectly clear?' He said the words quietly, but Camira had no doubt he meant every one of them.

She swallowed convulsively, her face as pale as her carnations.

'Good,' Marc said softly, and released her chin. 'For once you're without words.' He stood back and gestured with his arm. 'Will you enter my car, Miss Johnston? And don't bother about making any explanatory phone calls. He can sweat it out for a few hours.'

Camira stared blindly down at the narrow gold band on her finger. It didn't seem possible, and yet the impossible had happened. She had been married to Marc Riley an hour earlier and she was now back in the family unit in Surfer's Paradise, and the fact that he'd married her hadn't seemed to afford her new husband much pleasure at all. If anything, the opposite.

She turned jerkily as Marc strolled into the lounge. He threw his jacket over the back of a chair and loosened his tie. Then he crossed to the bar and poured two drinks.

He said as she took hers, 'You look as pale as you did the last time you arrived here. I hope you feel stronger. We have quite a day and a night—one way or the other—to get through.' He let his eyes roam over her impersonally, but the quick blush his words brought to her cheeks brought also a sudden glimpse of amusement to them.

'Sit down,' he said casually.

Camira hesitated, but when she sat he followed suit and said easily, 'I think I said something about letting you talk. Well, talk, Camira. You have my undivided attention. For the next ten minutes.'

It took her nearly all of that to assemble her scattered wits. She started several times, but nothing she wanted to say seemed to make the slightest sense.

Finally she said flatly, 'I don't understand why you've done this.'

'Strange,' he commented dryly, 'there's something I don't understand either. You've lied to someone down the line, but whoever it is, you're going to pay for it.'

'Wh-what do you mean?' she stammered, and raised a hand to her hot cheeks, suddenly seized with an incredible premonition.

'You allowed me to think you were still in love with David. You allowed him to think that. But you told Jane it was not so,' Marc said idly.

Camira opened and closed her mouth several times as her colour fluctuated. He lay back in his chair and observed her supreme discomfort with an ironic look.

She whispered finally, 'You mean Jane *told* you?'

'Uh-huh. She went to great lengths to track me down, as a matter of fact. I promised her I wouldn't tell you this, but then I thought, why not? Why shouldn't I?' He eyed her through half-closed lids. 'Perhaps we can talk now. Honestly for once. Perhaps you'd care to tell me just what's going on. What kind of a person you really are, Camira. And for your sake I hope it was Jane you told the truth to, otherwise you're going to have a life of misery from now on, married to the wrong man. Married,' he added evenly, 'in every sense of the word in the very near future.'

She said bitterly, 'I still don't understand. You don't trust me, you don't *like* me. You were only too relieved to be rid of me once your . . . lust cooled.' She stood up. 'As a matter of fact I do understand now. This is only revenge isn't it? Isn't it? You accused me of it,' she said on a rising note of hysteria, 'but it was really your ego that couldn't stand the blow, wasn't it? You couldn't bear to think that any girl, despite what she felt, could weigh it up against the odds and be able to walk away because she couldn't balance it. Could you?' she asked with a catch in her voice.

His dark eyes held hers captive as he said steadily, 'I'm prepared to admit to a feeling of pique, my dear Camira. But not because you were able to walk away from me. Only because you were prepared to prejudge me. Prepared for some inconceivable reason never to give me the slightest chance to prove myself. And as a final coup de grâce, prepared to go to a man you had no feeling for to make my rout complete. Believe me,' he said menacingly, 'that kind of cold-bloodedness deserves teaching a lesson, taking down a peg or two. I'm not a great fan of David Thorpe, but even he comes out of it slightly better than you do.'

He placed his drink carefully on the table and stood up. 'And the hour of reckoning is at hand, Camira,' he said huskily as he advanced towards her.

She stood her ground. 'I still doubt your motives,' she said tightly, 'if you'll forgive me for saying so.'

Marc grinned briefly, devilishly. 'Doubt away, sweetheart. All the doubts in the world aren't going to stop me from unearthing at least *one* truth now.'

Camira's nerve broke then all of a sudden and she turned to flee from him with her heart racing and a dry coppery taste of fear in her mouth. But in her blind flight, she tripped over the small table that had given her a bruised shin once before.

Marc's arms closed about her waist from behind. 'Whoa there!' he murmured as if to a recalcitrant filly. 'Thisaway, my love,' he added as he lifted her into his arms and she saw his white teeth flash in a wide grin. A grin that caused her to twist and turn in his arms and to flail at his strong, straight shoulders with her fists. But the end result of her struggles was to be tossed carelessly on to the bed in his bedroom, a room she had never entered before.

She lay there panting and trying to gather her breath as he deliberately closed the door and then strolled to the window to adjust the blinds so that the burning afternoon sun was blotted out leaving the room dim and cool.

'Right,' he said lazily as he turned to her. 'This thing usually goes one of two ways,' he said as he removed his tie and started to unbutton his shirt. 'You can go into a swoon of outraged maidenly modesty,' he raised his eyebrows quizzically as the shirt came off and he fingered the buckle of his belt, 'or you could facilitate the proceedings and certainly provide for the safety of your beautiful wedding dress by complying.'

She sat up. 'Complying!' she spat at him. 'Who would

advise me to comply with rape for the sake of a dress?'

'Rape?' he repeated ironically. 'Strong words, my dear. Let's just see, shall we?' He moved to the bed and loomed over her and she tensed convulsively as he took her shoulders in his hands. 'Don't put up a fight, Camira,' he warned softly. 'You've always wanted me as much as I've wanted you. And I can prove it.'

She stared into his eyes only inches from her own, captured suddenly not only by his hands but by the power she knew he would always hold over her. The power to cause her foolish body to be invaded by a trembling weakness at a mere glance. The power to evoke an incredible flood of sensuality and longing for him and him alone. And yet this was the man who had never once told her he loved her. The same man who was now only going to take her because he had discovered he had been duped.

She sagged suddenly beneath his hands and thought distractedly, I have one last weapon, but do I have the strength of mind and body to use it?

'That's better,' Marc murmured as he laid her back against the pillows. He smiled faintly, but she noticed a muscle move in his jaw as he said, 'Far better to be civilised about it. And while we're being such, perhaps you'd care to help me get you out of this dress. It might be better if you stood up.'

He stood up himself and held a hand down to her. She swallowed once and then obediently took his hand and allowed him to help her to her feet.

Marc undressed her slowly and carefully, article by article of clothing, and she turned alternately hot and cold beneath his hands until he stood back finally and said quietly, 'My God, you're beautiful, Camira. Even more so than I thought. No,' he shook his head as she started to bring her arms up to cover her breasts. 'No,' he said again. She lowered her arms, unable to meet his hazel gaze, until he moved closer and tipped her chin upwards with his fingers. 'More beautiful than even I thought,' he said again with just a trace of unsteadiness. His fingers left her chin and he drew her into his arms and lifted her on to the bed. Camira closed her eyes as he turned away briefly, aware that her control was slipping already. But she made one last valiant effort as she felt the bed sag slightly beneath his weight, felt his hands on her breasts with a featherlight touch, cupping them gently, and then his mouth where his hands had been as he gathered her into his arms and he was stroking her and trailing his fingers down the slender length of her back and every square inch of her skin felt incredibly alive and tingling with pure erotic sensation.

Then she heard him laugh deep in his throat. 'Oh, Camira,' he breathed into one ear, and probed the delicate skin behind it with his tongue. 'I might have known you were still fighting! So be it, sweetheart. Hold out as long as you can, but I promise you, it won't be long.'

And all the sensations she'd felt till then paled before the practised expertise he now brought to bear on her body with his hands and his mouth, until she abandoned herself to the sheer unbearable delight of it with a low moan, uncaring of incurring that mocking amusement or of anything beyond the driving need to give herself to him completely.

But it wasn't amusement she saw at the last moment on his face as he lifted his head and murmured, 'It's now or never, Camira.'

'Oh yes!' she pleaded. 'Please, yes. . . .'

But the delight was tempered with pain that she couldn't hide, didn't want to hide, and she finally lay still in his arms with tears on her cheeks and yet a feeling of elation in her heart. For whatever might come she could never regret giving Marc Riley the supreme gift she had to bestow. For whatever might come, she thought hazily, and tensed herself suddenly as he uttered a groan of—was it despair?—and gathered her more closely to him.

'Camira,' he murmured her name over and over again as he kissed her tears, kissed her eyelids and cradled her body in a delicate, gentle embrace. 'Can you ever forgive me?' he said huskily. 'I think I've loved you since I first laid eyes on you. Loved you not only for the way you look, which incidentally has been a source of sheer torment, but for your fierce independence—everything about you. The fact that you're the only girl I think I've ever met that I could take my hat off to and say I admire and respect you as much as any man. Look at me, Camira—my only love.'

Her eyes fluttered open with an expression of wary incredulity in them and he buried his dark head in her breast with another groan.

'Marc,' she whispered, and touched his hair lightly. He lifted his head and she felt as if she would drown in his hazel glance. 'Say that again,' she whispered shakily.

'Do you really want to hear it, Camira?' he murmured on a note of self-directed irony. 'I've abused you in every way, and now physically. And the fact that I've—satisfied myself that you were a virgin—if nothing else it proves what a heel I am. I hurt you, more or less in cold blood. Can you forgive that?' he asked somberly.

'I wanted you to,' she said, and permitted a tiny ray of hope to enter her heart. She traced the outline of his jaw with one fingertip. 'You were right about one thing,' she added with a small tremulous smile. 'I've always wanted you. I think . . . what happened to my parents, not only that but losing everything like that made me . . . I don't know—*afraid* to feel too strongly for anything. That's. . . .'

'I know,' he said quietly. 'I knew that from very early on. But ever since I met you it's as if all the demons in hell have been on my back. And you were right too, Camira. It was an incredible blow to my ego when you walked away from me. That, plus the sheer pain of not really knowing what Thorpe meant to you. It was almost too much.' He amended that. 'It was too much. I . . . I think I went a little mad. I used Lisa shamefully too.'

He stared at her and that muscle moved in his jaw again. 'Perhaps I should explain about Lisa—all the Lisas I've known.'

'You don't have to,' said Camira with a tiny quirk to her lips. 'I've already had it explained to me by an expert.'

He raised his eyebrows. 'Who?'

'Tim.'

He started to speak, but stopped and caught her fingers instead. 'Oh,' he said finally as he kissed each finger separately. He grinned suddenly. 'I kinda had the feeling my family and staff were solidly on your side. But,' he sobered, 'in my own defence perhaps I should say this. I wasn't the first and I won't be the last for Lisa. She's a survivor, and I don't mean to knock her when I say that. Because you see I thought I was too. I thought I could put a pair of cool grey eyes out of my head with little trouble. Instead I found your hold was so strong on me that I had to resort to caveman tactics when I realised I couldn't live without you.'

She moved in the circle of his arms, revelling in the feeling of them. 'We owe Jane a large debt of gratitude,' she murmured with a lurking smile. 'I bet she's worried sick right now, though.'

Marc kissed her forehead. 'As a matter of fact she's not, my darling. You see the reason she had so much trouble contacting me was because I was already on my way home and intent on plucking you out of David Thorpe's arms. Her news only added fuel to the flame so to speak. But I think she was relieved all the same. She only did what she did after a whole lot of heart searching and still with much trepidation. She's a good friend,' he added softly. 'Camira,' his eyes were dark and intent now. 'Camira, the way you're lying in my arms now, does that mean—you've forgiven me?'

She nodded gravely. 'Provided, Marc, that you'll forgive me for being so stupid?' She stared at him with a look of shy wonder in her eyes. 'Will you?'

He crushed her to him. 'Forgive you?' he said huskily. 'There's nothing to forgive my love. And,' he hesitated, 'it won't always be so painful, I promise you. In fact the very next time will be a lot better for you.'

'Good,' she murmured demurely. 'Could it be . . . soon, Mr Riley?'

'It could, Mrs Riley. Indeed,' his eyes glinted at her, 'seeing that we're so positioned, how about—right now? Hell!' He sat up suddenly.

'What is it?' she asked anxiously.

'Thorpe,' he said briefly. 'I don't know, but suddenly I feel more charitable towards him. Perhaps we should put him out of his misery.'

'Marc!' She caught his hand as he went to get up. He turned to her.

'I'm so glad you told me that it wasn't Jane who . . . brought you to me. And in a little way I can repay that. You see, David knows. Not this,' she drew her hands along his shoulders, 'but I rang him this morning just before you came. I told him I couldn't marry him and why. I . . . I think he understood. I . . . I couldn't do it even though I thought I'd killed every spark of feeling you had for me. Oh, Marc!' she said with tears in her eyes again, 'I. . . .'

But whatever it was she had been going to say was smothered in his embrace. An embrace that grew more urgent by the minute. 'Dear God, I love you, Camira,' he said finally, as shaken as she was by the intensity of their emotions. 'Are you're sure you're ready for me? We can take this slowly, you know. We have all the time in the world.'

'We shouldn't waste it talking too much, then,' she murmured languidly with a finger on his lips. 'You did say you weren't a great one for words, didn't you?'

THE SPORT OF THE ELITE

Among sportsmen, polo is regarded as one of the toughest games to play. It takes great strength and skill to master this age-old sport, in which players atop swift-charging horses try to hit a bamboo ball through the goalposts with bamboo mallets. But skill alone is not enough to qualify one for the competitive ranks. For polo is almost exclusively the preserve of the very wealthy, boasting such notable enthusiasts as Prince Charles of England. Considering the expense of maintaining a fleet of sturdy polo ponies—a must for the players as the game is extremely arduous—it's no wonder! In fact, polo has been the domain of the nobility ever since its ancient beginnings in Persia in the first century A.D.

Initially a rough warlike spectacle, polo was used as a training method for the Persian king's guard, the elite cavalry unit. Later it was played extensively by the Persian nobility, including the women. The popular game soon spread eastward to the Orient, where it suffered its most tragic day to date. In A.D. 910 the accidental death of a favorite relative in a polo match prompted Emperor T'ai Tsu of China to order all the surviving players beheaded!

Centuries later the game was still going strong. British tea planters in India latched onto polo in the mid-1800s, then passed their addiction on to British troops stationed there at the time. From India it was an easy jump to England and the rest of the western world. Today polo is a highly organized and regulated sport in Argentina, the United States, South Africa, England, Mexico, Chile, Australia, Hong Kong, India and many other nations.

Harlequin Presents...

Stories to dream about...
Stories of love...

...all-consuming, passionate love,
the way you've always imagined it,
the way you know it should be!

Choose from this list of
Harlequin Romance editions.*

975	**Sister of the Housemaster** Eleanor Farnes	1178	**Rendezvous in Lisbon** Iris Danbury
978	**Kind and Gentle Is She** Margaret Malcolm	1182	**Golden Apple Island** Jane Arbor
991	**Charity Child** Sara Seale	1189	**Accidental Bride** Susan Barrie
1150	**The Bride of Mingalay** Jean S. MacLeod	1190	**The Shadow and the Sun** Amanda Doyle
1152	**A Garland of Marigolds** Isobel Chace	1193	**The Heights of Love** Belinda Dell
1154	**You Can't Stay Here** Barbara Gilmour	1197	**Penny Plain** Sara Seale
1157	**Yesterday's Magic** Jane Arbor	1199	**Johnny Next Door** Margaret Malcolm
1158	**The Valley of Aloes** Wynne May	1211	**Bride of Kylsaig** Iris Danbury
1159	**The Gay Gordons** Barbara Allen	1212	**Hideway Heart** Roumelia Lane
1164	**Meadowsweet** Margaret Malcolm	1226	**Honeymoon Holiday** Elizabeth Hoy
1165	**Ward of Lucifer** Mary Burchell	1228	**The Young Nightingales** Mary Whistler
1166	**Dolan of Sugar Hills** Kate Starr	1233	**A Love of Her Own** Hilda Pressley
1171	**The Wings of Memory** Eleanor Farnes	1246	**The Constant Heart** Eleanor Farnes
1174	**The English Tutor** Sara Seale	1494	**The Valley of Illusion** Ivy Ferrari
1176	**Winds of Enchantment** Rosalind Brett	1605	**Immortal Flower** Elizabeth Hoy

Some of these book were originally published under different titles.